# Order of th

## Book 1: Rebellion

### Alex Keller

# Order of the Furnace
# Book 1: Rebellion

First published by Mogzilla in 2015

Paperback edition:
ISBN: 9781906132316
Text copyright Alex Keller
Cover by Andrew Minchin.
Cover ©Mogzilla 2015

Printed in the UK

http://www.mogzilla.co.uk/orderofthefurnace

# Prologue

*Not today. I won't die today. I promise.*

Slowly, ever so slowly, Lena Faran made her way, on her stomach, through the dark, damp grass at the foot of Castle Winlow wondering if her next breath would be her last.

Lena was a squire in the Order of the Furnace and over the past few years she had found herself in many life-threatening situations. However, right now she was hard pressed to remember anything quite as grim as what she was doing now.

Castle Winlow, the rebel stronghold, towered over her, brutal and grey. Lena pressed herself to the ground and inched forward, feeling as if a million eyes were on her, watching and waiting for the perfect moment to strike and whisk her life away.

She carried on regardless, checking the ground for traps and other devices that could cause problems during the coming fight. She reached forward and felt a wooden stake coming out of the ground which, if left, may hurt a horse or soldier. She grabbed hold of it and pulled. *Come on!*

After a brief struggle the stake came loose. Lena pulled it out of the ground and slid it into the bag on her back with the rest she had discovered. She moved on. Mud oozed into the gaps of her thick clothes; she would have groaned if she could make any noise...

Then, without warning...*THUNK!*

An arrow hit the ground next to her; its wooden shaft only a short distance from her face.

Lena froze; her heart in her mouth.

*No!*

# Chapter One

Earlier that night, Lena stood outside her tent and felt the spring wind bite her face; it made her shiver. She gritted her teeth, crossed her arms over herself, and rubbed her shoulders for a little warmth while she looked around the army camp.

It was barely past midnight and the camp was lit by a thousand glowing lanterns, torches and fires. Despite the time, the camp was still a loud, chaotic place brimming with activity. Lena could hear the blacksmiths' hammers crashing onto anvils, teamsters crying out to one another and soldiers, marching up and down in procession.

Lena looked to her left and saw one of the Order knights passing by, whose golden mechanical armour hissed and clanked, leaving deep foot-prints in the ground. When the knight saw Lena, she raised her arm and waved.

'Sir Poland's looking for you,' the knight called out.

Lena waved back. 'Thanks, I'll go to him.'

'Good luck!' said the knight, stomping off in the opposite direction.

Lena left her squires' tent and made her way through the camp to the kitchens a short distance away, yawning as she went. As she got closer the aroma of baking bread and crackling bacon replaced the usual camp smells of manure and sweat.

The kitchen itself consisted of a simple, long wooden table covered in food behind which were greasy-aproned cooks stirring massive pots, checking spitting frying pans and pulling steaming loaves out of ovens. Lena's mouth watered.

When Lena arrived at the kitchen she grabbed a hunk of warm bread from the table and one of the cooks' assistants handed her a mug of sweet tea. She thanked the assistant, turned away and blew on the tea, watching as the steam swirled in front of her. She took a sip and a bite from the bread, and then left the kitchen feeling better for something hot in her stomach.

Ten minutes later she arrived at the squires' mustering post on the other side of the camp where she saw her lord and master, Sir Alberghast Poland.

Sir Poland, the knight-commander of the Order of the Furnace, was standing tall and proud and already in his magnificent, ornate armour. In his gauntleted hands were pieces of paper. He looked at each in turn with his brow furrowed.

'Milord,' said Lena.

'Ah, Lena,' said Sir Poland. He raised his bushy, silver eyebrows, briefly revealing his bright eyes beneath before they returned to the papers. 'There you are.'

'You needed me?'

'Yes, yes,' Sir Poland replied gruffly. 'You're scouting no-man's land this morning.'

'Okay. Who's with me?'

'Davos, Benji, Aisha, Berry, Xander and Ana. You'll need to gather them.'

'I'm leading?'

Sir Poland shook his head. 'Not this time. It's Berry's turn.'

'Really?' replied Lena. 'But last time-'

Sir Poland frowned. 'Berry needs the experience more than you do. She's been on the side-lines long enough.'

'But... Lena wanted to stomp her foot but she resisted. She was too old for that sort of thing and Sir Poland hated it.

'Leave it, Lena,' said Sir Poland. 'It's in the past and she's learned her lesson.'

Lena sighed and gave up arguing; she could see the old knight had made up his mind. 'Where is she?' she asked.

'In her tent, I imagine,' said Sir Poland.

'I just came from there!'

'And now you can go back. You have your orders.'

Lena saluted her knight commander and left in a huff.

'And less of that attitude!' cried Sir Poland.

# Chapter Two

Lena made her way towards the second squire's tent. When she arrived there was a crowd outside. They were all peering in with the occasional gasp and *ooooh!*

'What's going on?' Lena asked the boy closest to her. It was Silas.

'Erik's upset Berry,' Silas replied.

Lena had known Silas Anderson for her entire time with the Order as he had joined the same month as she did. Silas was a quiet boy and a good ally in a fight. He had grown up on the streets of Jultsthorne: a huge, dangerous city in the East of the Empire. He was short for his age, only coming up to Lena's shoulder, but this wasn't a disadvantage; his height meant it was just harder to hit him on the battlefield.

'Lena sighed. 'Let me through!' she called out.

The other squires moved out of the way and Lena stepped through the canvas.

Like her own tent, this tent contained row upon row of beds, enough to sleep fifty squires. It was neat and orderly, although the two squires screaming at each other on the floor near the entrance meant it was less orderly than normal.

Lena saw that Berry had pinned Erik to the ground. Two other squires were trying to pull Berry off but they weren't having much luck.

'Call me that, again!' shouted Berry. 'Come on, say it!'

Berry had Erik's collar in one hand and a cruel-looking knife in the other. Erik had managed to get hold of Berry's wrist but the knife was getting closer nonetheless.

Lena raised her voice: 'Berry, we don't have time for this!' But

Berry ignored her. Lena tutted and saw the knife was now touching the skin on Erik's neck. She turned to Silas.

'What happened?'

Silas grinned. 'Berry was waking everyone up and Erik wanted longer in bed. She hit Erik with the flat of her sword to get him moving and she told him if he didn't the next whack will be with the edge.'

'I bet he didn't like that.'

'Nope.'

'So he..?'

'Yep.' Silas tried to keep himself from laughing.

Lena sighed again. It was too early for this.

'Get off me!' yelled Erik at Berry. 'You're mad!'

'Don't call me that then!' screamed Berry. 'You know I *hate* it!'

'I didn't say anything!'

'Yes you did!'

'What did I say?'

'You know what!'

'No!'

Lena went over to Berry and Erik and waved away the two squires who were trying to help. She knelt down.

'Come on, Berry, we've got things to do.'

Berry turned her head and looked at Lena.

'What?' Her eyes were wide and manic.

'Work. Us. Leave him alone,' said Lena.

'But-!'

'Sir Poland's orders. We're scouting. You're in charge.'

'*I'm* in charge?' The anger in Berry's face faded to happy surprise. 'But what about last time?'

'No one was seriously hurt,' said Lena. Come on, we need to go. And I don't think Sir Poland would be pleased if he heard about all this.' She looked at Erik who had gone quiet while she and Berry spoke.

Berry let go of Erik's clothes and he slumped to the floor.

'Okay…' she said. She stood up, brushing herself down, and Erik, now free, scrambled away.

'Go on, *Strawberry*,' said Erik. 'Run away.'

The temperature in the tent dropped a few degrees and all eyes turned on Berry.

Berry Weyman's parents had wanted Berry and her sisters to be the sort of children who play musical instruments, paint pretty pictures and take an interest in clothes, so they gave them names they thought would be suitable for these pursuits. Unfortunately, Berry and her sisters: Daisy, Peach and Petal, had all found swords, chain mail, danger and dirt far more interesting than pianos and watercolours. Daisy and Petal had become bloodthirsty mercenaries, fighting for whoever paid them the most, while Peach was last seen hunting in the deadly jungles of Pala five years ago. She had not been seen since.

Berry glanced at Lena. 'Now, I can't ignore that can I?'

Lena looked at Erik and frowned at him. 'Fine,' she said to Berry. 'But be quick.'

Lena and Berry left the squires' tent minutes later with Erik howling within.

# Chapter Three

'So what are we doing?' asked Berry as she and Lena walked through the camp. 'Great!' she said sarcastically after Lena had told her. 'I'd rather clean out the horses. At least I won't get shot at there.'

'Same here,' said Lena. 'But orders are orders.'

Lena and Berry saw the other scouts waiting for them at the edge of the camp. They greeted each other and made their way towards Castle Winlow. Ahead, Lena could see tiny dots of light shining from the battlements of the castle: torches of soldiers that, from this distance, looked like fireflies.

'Spread out,' ordered Berry when they were close enough to do their work. The scouts fanned out until they were about ten metres away from each other.

'You know what to do,' said Berry.

'Aye,' came a chorus of hushed voices.

Lena crouched down and began to slowly shuffle slowly toward the far-away walls of the rebel castle.

****

*THUNK!!*

Lena stayed where she was for a few seconds more.

Her mind raced, her heart beat loudly in her chest, and her eyes fixed on the arrow in front of her.

*This is bad,* she thought. *This is really bad...*

Thankfully, the arrow wasn't on fire. It must have gone out either on its way down or when it hit the dirt.

It meant they couldn't see her from above right now; but had they seen her before it went out?

*What should I do? Come on, think!*

Lena decided to stay where she was. She hadn't heard any shouts from the battlements and if she moved straight away the soldiers above might see her. Lena waited, squeezed her eyes shut and braced for the next arrow. It never came.

Lena sighed with relief. *That was close!*

She began crawling once again. She kept going, pushing forward. Her heart was still being fast but she had caught her breath at least and could think clearly again.

Finally, Lena reached Castle Winlow's curtain wall. She stood up and put her back against it, staying in the shadows and out of sight.

'Find anything?' hissed a voice from the darkness. Lena tensed but it was just Berry.

'Stakes; a few traps. Nothing much,' Lena replied. 'You?'

The shadow shifted and Berry appeared.

'Same,' said Berry.

'How are the others?' asked Lena.

Benji and Ana found bear traps.

'Are they okay?'

'Benji is.'

Both squires were silent for a time. Ana had only been with the Order for a couple of years but it was still hard losing another squire.

'Okay,' said Lena. 'We'd best carry on.'

Berry turned to leave. 'Keep going,' she said over her shoulder. 'I'll see you back at camp.' And with that Berry slid off down the wall like a ghost, leaving Lena alone.

Lena took five steps left and looked out over no-man's land again. She then got down on her belly once more and started crawling away from the castle.

She would have to make the trip back and forth another ten times tonight.

# Chapter Four

When Lena had finished her duties she made her way, dirty, stinking, cold and wet, back to the army camp. Dawn was breaking and sunlight glinted off halberds, pikes and helmets; birds sang in the trees. It could almost be a nice day, Lena thought.

She called out the day's password, walked past the forward defenses and into the camp proper. It was busier now as final preparations were underway. She went back to her tent where she washed and changed. When she had finished cleaning up she left and looked for Sir Poland again.

Lena caught sight of the old knight coming out of one of the Order's pavilions.

Lena moved forward quickly, darting between soldiers with the occasional '*hey!*' and '*oi!*' being shouted at her whenever one of her feet landed on someone else's. When she got closer, she saw Sir Poland looked worried.

'Anything wrong, Milord?' she asked.

'Lena,' said Sir Poland, his voice like ice. 'Go to the marshals. Tell them to prepare. We fight within the hour.'

'Yes, sir,' replied Lena. She turned to go but then hesitated. She knew what she about to do was against the rules, but she had known Sir Poland for a long time and he always said he wanted her to think for herself.

'What's happened?' she asked.

'Something doesn't feel right about all this,' said the old knight.

'In what way, Milord?'

'We've been away from the kingdom for two years now

and something has changed, I can feel it. Duke Winlow has always been loyal to the crown. It is very odd for him to rebel like this.'

Lena looked at Sir Poland but remained silent.

'It's no matter,' the knight continued. 'Go, do what must be done.' Sir Poland waved Lena away.

Lena went to each knight-marshal in turn to relay her master's commands. She saw the Moles' engines roar into life; the auto-trebuchets loaded; the ballistae bound into position like excited dogs; and the siege towers unfold themselves until they cast great shadows over the camp. It was impressive no matter how many times she saw it and she was sure it must strike fear into the hearts of anyone they fought.

'We're ready,' said Lena as she entered Sir Poland's tent once again. She saw Sir Poland checking his armour a final time.

'Good,' replied the old knight. He paused, turned, and looked Lena over. 'Now, this is an important day for you, is it not? Are you ready for your first proper battle?'

Despite the years of training and studying, Lena knew what she was about to do was very dangerous. She was strong, a good rider and well-practiced with swords, spears and all manner of weapons; but she had seen the result of many battles as the squire of Sir Poland: the cuts and wounds, the dents, bruises and much, much worse. She had come close to death on quite a few occasions without even being in a battle, but all that would be nothing compared with what was about to come.

'I think so,' Lena replied.

'I can't hear you, squire!' said Sir Poland. 'I asked you if you were ready!'

Lena clenched her fists and looked Sir Poland in the eye. 'Yes, sir!' she cried.

Sir Poland smiled through his bushy beard.

'That's more like it. There's no shame in being afraid, Lena, but when the time comes I know you will do well; I don't doubt that. Keep going the way you are and you will be *Lady* Faran in no time at all.'

'Thank you, Milord.' Only knights of the realm were called Sir or Lady and Lena couldn't wait to be one herself. It would be a great honour.

'Remember, your brothers and sisters will always be nearby and I'll be keeping watch too,' Sir Poland continued.

'I know, Milord,' Lena replied. 'I'll try to stay alive.'

'See that you do.'

'What will I be doing?' Lena asked.

'You'll be with me in the vanguard of course.'

Lena's heart sunk. Sir Poland was always one of the first into battle and the last to leave. Today was going to be even harder than she had been expecting.

'But we need you kitted out first,' said Sir Poland.

'Go and find Kruger. He should be waiting for you.'

# Chapter Five

Lena left Sir Poland's tent and, trembling only ever so slightly, walked towards the other squires who had gathered nearby.

When she got closer she saw Berry and Silas. Berry was already in her armour and practicing her sword swing while Silas stood next to her. Even though the siege of Castle Winlow would be Silas' first battle too, he looked nowhere near as nervous as Lena felt.

'Over here!' Berry shouted and Lena went over to her friends.

'Tell her,' hissed Silas to Berry. 'Go on.'

'What is it?' Lena asked.

'Look over there.' Berry moved her head slightly. 'The Vulture's turned up again.'

A few hundred feet away, on top of a rise, Lena saw Grand Minister Erin, King Claudio's special advisor. She was standing with a retinue of her personal guard and dressed in her usual black clothes. Her shoulders were hunched and she stood motionless, looking thoughtful. Erin was one of the most powerful people in the kingdom and also the head of the Jasareen, the King's assassins, which made a lot of people even more nervous around her for very obvious reasons.

'She gives me the creeps,' said Berry, pushing her sword back into its sheath with a grunt. 'She just stands there and watches as if we're here to entertain her. This is the third time she's shown her face in as many months.'

'She *is* allowed to be here,' replied Silas.

'I know,' said Berry. 'But it's like she's perched on our

shoulders. It's weird. What's she worried about? It's not as if we're going to disappear on her.'

'I think something odd might be going on,' said Lena. 'Sir Poland was a bit worried earlier. Something isn't right about this fight.'

'What do you mean?' asked Silas.

'I don't know,' Lena replied. 'Maybe it's nothing.'

'The Duke's a rebel,' said Berry, shrugging her shoulders. 'And we protect the kingdom from threats. It doesn't say anywhere our own people can't be the threat. We'll fight whoever we have to.'

'I know,' said Lena, but she didn't feel convinced.

Before they could carry on, Kruger, the squire-master, interrupted them. He marched up to the squires and loomed over them, peering through the nest of scars that crisscrossed his face

'You lot!' Kruger shouted. 'Stop wasting time. You're here to fight, not socialize. Lena, Silas, come with me. The rest of you, get your things together and report back here in fifteen minutes. It's time.'

Silas and Lena followed the squire-master into a nearby pavilion. Inside, many of the Order's weapons and armour could be found. Kruger pointed to two clothes-horses covered in metal plates.

'Get them on, gather your weapons, and meet me outside with the others. Quickly now.'

'Yes, sir,' replied Lena and Silas together.

Kruger left and the squires helped each other into their battle-dress. It wasn't anywhere near as good as a knight's armour but it should keep them safe enough for the next few hours.

'Are you ready?' asked Silas as he buckled Lena's cuirass. The locks of the armour hissed as they connected.

'I think so,' said Lena. 'You?'

Lena turned and saw that Silas now looked very worried.

'I'm a bit scared,' said Silas. 'If I'm honest.'

'It'll be all right,' Lena replied as calmly as she could.

'Really?'

'Sure. We're the Order of the Furnace after all. Remember what we've been taught and stay close to the others. Just stay alive.'

Silas nodded. 'Thanks, Lena. I will.'

They finished dressing, took their weapons and went back outside. They found Kruger standing in front of the other squires with a list in his hands.

'Silas Anderson, Michael Obasi, Ton Singh and Sebastien Delure, you'll be in the Moles,' barked Kruger. 'Berry Weyman, Lena Faran and Thomas and Gregory Delure, you'll be in the vanguard. The rest of you will be manning the siege towers with me.'

The squire-master paused and looked over his charges.

'Any questions? No? Good. You know where to go. Dismissed.'

Berry nudged Lena in the side.

'Looks like we're together,' said Berry. 'Come on, let's get ready. This'll be *fun!*'

Lena was almost certain it wouldn't be.

# Chapter Six

Lena sat on her piebald horse and watched the battle begin.

The auto-trebuchets rumbled into place and started hurling great rocks at the castle walls and the ballistae-hounds ran from position to position, firing their bolts then moving on as their missiles flew through the air. Castle Winlow's walls could barely be seen with all the dust and debris flung into the air.

After a time, it looked as if the rebel castle had been weakened enough to start the assault. The siege engines stopped and Lena tensed. It would be their turn soon.

'Bring the Bull!' cried Sir Poland.

Lena watched as the Bull, a massive soul-machine covered in pistons and steel that seemed to run on rage alone, strode forward towards the main gates of castle Winlow.

It lowered its head and charged.

Boom! Boom! Boom!

The ground shook with the Bull's footfalls followed by an almighty crash as the Bull's horns hit the castle gates. Lena's horse whinnied at the noise and she patted its neck to quieten it down.

'There, there,' said Lena into the horse's ear.

The Bull turned, walked away, and charged again. The wooden beams of the gate were giving way, bending and breaking inwards, then cracking under the onslaught.

'As soon as the Bull is through we advance,' said Sir Poland.

Lena turned to see Sir Poland sitting on Pandora, his Archon. Pandora shone in the morning sun, proud, magnificent, and bigger than the largest war-horse. Like the Bull, Pandora was a soul-machine; she contained the spirit of an animal but her body was made of metal and mechanical parts. Pandora could run all day without getting tired and carry a knight in full battle-armour and never slow down. Lena hoped one day she would ride an Archon into battle, but for now she could only imagine what it would be like.

There was a loud crash and Lena felt the horse underneath her tense as the Bull smashed through the gate in a cloud of dust. Moments later, it reappeared again and stepped aside, snorting and shaking its head.

It was Lena and the vanguard's turn now. She looked to Sir Poland.

'Here we go,' said Sir Poland to Lena quietly. He winked at her and then, in a much louder voice, called out: 'For King Claudio, brothers and sisters! Charge!'

The siege engines of the Royal Army and the Order went quiet and the vanguard geed up their horses and Archons. They stampeded into Winlow castle's courtyard, passing the Bull, the broken gate, and rubble that now made up the castle's entrance.

Inside, Lena looked up and caught sight of Duke Winlow's soldiers scattering and looking for cover. An odd feeling came over her: she found herself feeling sorry for them. Her own fear had now gone; the ride had made her excited and eager, as if nothing could stop her, and she now understood: while she was scared, those she was about to fight were just as scared as she was, if not more so.

'Halt! Dismount!' cried Sir Poland once the vanguard was within the castle courtyard.

Lena's training kicked in. She slid off her horse, drew her sword and readied her shield, as did the rest of the vanguard. They were like a well-oiled machine; unstoppable.

'Hold!' ordered Sir Poland.

Lena was tense, ready to fight; but when she peered over her shield she saw the courtyard had emptied of Duke Winlow's soldiers. They had disappeared behind overturned carts, hay bales and anything else they could find. Lena felt strangely disappointed. Behind her she heard the horses and Archons ride back to safety.

Then she saw the bows.

'Winlow knows us well,' Lena heard Sir Poland mutter.

'Defend!' he called out to the Vanguard. 'Position three!'

Lena huddled together with rest of the vanguard. They sheathed their swords and raised their shields over their heads or pushed them forward as one. Their shields clicked together, turning the knights and squires standing in the courtyard into what looked like a huge metal turtle.

'Brace!'

A moment later, Lena could feel arrows thudding into her shield. They made her arms ache. She crouched down further and pushed her shoulder against the shield to soften the blows.

'Ready counter-measures!' shouted Sir Poland.

*Our turn,* thought Lena.

Lena reached up and within her shield found two buttons. She pressed one and waited.

'Fire!'

Lena pressed the second button and heard a rush of air. On the other side of her shield small bolts hidden in the central hub uncovered and fired outward. The bolts entered the air around the knights filling it like a dark cloud. It would expand very quickly, spraying the deadly bolts all over the courtyard in every direction.

She could hear cries; the bolts had done their job.

Lena was about to unlock her shield when she felt a nudge. 'Wait for it,' said Berry who had taken position next to Lena.

From behind them came the heavy pounding of the

ballistae-hounds running through the castle gates. They took up positions behind the vanguard and started firing their six-foot bolts at the defenders. Once the first detachment had done its job they moved away, letting another detachment take their place. This continued for a few minutes and Lena noticed she hadn't felt any arrows hit her shield for a while.

Then Lena heard another voice far above her.

'Clear!'

Lena hit a switch that opened a small viewing panel in her shield. Above, she could see Kruger on the battlements waving down at them.

The siege towers had been successful. Those in the towers had done their work and pushed the defenders off the walls and into the main keep. Lena relaxed a little. The first part of the battle had been won and she'd barely done anything.

'That went well-' began Berry.

There was a rumble; terrible and deep under their feet. The ground shifted. Lena staggered, barely able to keep upright.

'Oh no...' She groaned. Berry steadied her. She looked around and saw smoke appear from some nearby doorways. 'No, no, no...!'

The Moles.

'Vanguard,' said Sir Poland; his face now cold and terrible. 'With me.'

Lena and the rest of the vanguard ran to one of the smoking doorways littered around the castle courtyard. Once there, Sir Poland peered inside.

'Duke Winlow has done something,' said the old knight. 'Quick, follow me.' Sir Poland disappeared through the doorway and the rest followed.

Lena hoped Silas and the others were all right.

# Chapter Seven

The vanguard raced down into the depths of Winlow castle. They clanked down the stairs, following the smoke that rolled along the ceilings above them. Lena could feel heat on her face, making sweat run into her eyes.

When they reached the bottom, the stairwell opened out into something out of a nightmare.

Lena spluttered and looked on, dumbstruck. Fire seemed to hang in the air and crawl up the walls as if the stone itself was alight. It was horrible. Smoke billowed, making Lena cough and splutter.

'Over there!' cried Sir Poland.

Lena looked to where the old knight was pointing. At the far end of a long, vaulted cellar, through the smoke, she saw the Moles. They were blackened and some were still on fire. *Silas...*

'Snap out of it!' shouted Sir Poland. He nudged Lena forward. 'Get in there and help!'

Lena nodded and ran down the length of the cellar. As she went she held her hand over her mouth, trying to keep the smoke out. The closer she got the more the heat beat at her and her armour felt heavier and heavier.

When Lena arrived she saw the first Mole was completely out of the ground and its hatches were open; Lena guessed it must have been the first to arrive. The machine's sides were now scarred black and it was terribly damaged. She stopped and started to peer inside.

'Not that one,' said Sir Poland coming up right behind her. 'Move on.'

Lena turned, puzzled. Then she caught a smell; like something from a kitchen at dinner time.

*No...*

'Go,' said the old knight sternly.

Lena went to the second Mole. It looked in better shape than the first. When Lena got closer she could hear moaning inside.

'There are survivors in here!' she called back to the others.

She pulled the emergency release and the cabin door opened. She looking inside she saw a number of knights and squires, including Silas.

Lena climbed into the Mole and started pulling her comrades free one by one. Most were still conscious and, with a little help, could find their way out on their own once the straps holding them in their seats had been undone or cut. But when Lena got to Silas she could see her friend's eyes were closed and he wasn't moving.

'Come on, Silas...'

Lena bent down, placed her ear to Silas' chest and then cried out with relief. Silas was still breathing and his heart was beating. Lena undid the straps that covered his chest, but when she tried to move him his armour made him too heavy. She reached down and unbuckled the same armour she had helped put on only a short time before. It fell away with a clank.

'...Lena?' Silas mumbled. He coughed harshly.

Lena looked up to see Silas' eyes were open. 'It's okay. I'll have you out of here soon.'

'What...what happened? Where am I?'

'We're under Castle Winlow. The Duke had set some kind of trap.'

'I remember. The others?'

Lena shrugged. 'I don't know.'

Silas nodded and Lena pulled her friend free. He helped as

much as he could and they made it to the Mole's exit into the waiting arms of Lady Openden, Silas' own master.

'He's alive,' Lena gasped, her lungs now straining at the lack of oxygen in the hellish cellar.

'You did well,' said Lady Openden. 'I'll take care of him. Go. Sir Poland needs you.'

Lena looked at Silas and hesitated.

'That's an order,' said Lady Openden. 'Go.' She slung Silas' arm over her shoulder helped him to the cellar exit.

Lena went back to the first Mole and saw Sir Poland emerging from within; he looked sick. When he caught Lena's eye he quickly turned and closed the hatch behind him.

'Did anyone survive, Milord?' Lena began.

Sir Poland shook his head.

'No.'

'How did this happen?' asked Lena.

'Winlow must have flooded the cellars with marsh gas,' said Sir Poland. 'All it took was one spark. The second Mole must have caused it after the first had landed. Their door was open when the gas ignited. They didn't stand a chance. It could have brought the whole castle down though. Winlow must be desperate.'

Lena shuddered at the thought of what happened to those in the first Mole and then at the thought of Silas' being crushed as the castle collapsed.

'Come with me,' said Sir Poland.

Sir Poland and Lena made their way back up the stairs, emerging into the courtyard once again. After the horror of the cellars Lena almost forgot she was in a battle. She breathed the fresh air deeply only to be then pulled roughly against the wall by her master.

'Are you mad, girl?' cried Sir Poland. 'Keep you head down at all times. We're not safe yet.'

As if to prove his point, an arrow smashed into the paving

stone where Lena had just stood.

Sir Poland lent forward. 'Winlow!' he cried, looking up at the Keep and cupping his hands around his mouth. 'I know you can hear me! Surrender now or I will tear your castle down with you inside it!'

The castle went quiet. The siege held its breath.

Then a voice came from high in the Keep.

'Who are you?'

'Alberghast Poland, Knight Commander of the Order of the Furnace.'

'The Duke wants to speak to you,' said the voice. 'Just you. No one else…please.'

Sir Poland paused. 'Tell your men to stand down,' he said finally. My squire will join me and if anyone tries to attack us I'll have their head, understand?'

Lena looked at her master wide-eyed. She could barely breathe, she was covered head to foot in soot and could only just about see out of her burning eyes.

'You're my back-up,' said Sir Poland.

# Chapter Eight

There was a scraping noise and Lena saw the bolt-ridden doors of Castle Winlow's keep creak open. A man's head appeared. He looked at Sir Poland and Lena nervously before beckoning them inside.

'Stay with me,' said Sir Poland. 'I think we'll be safe enough for now.'

Lena nodded. She and Sir Poland climbed the steps of the Keep and went through the doors.

On the other side of the doors Lena found scared-looking men and women huddled against the Keep's walls, all watching both her and Sir Poland fearfully. As Lena and Sir Poland moved on, the soldiers would shy away from them and wouldn't meet Lena's eye. Lena also noticed there was something odd about them; about the way they stood and the way they held their weapons. None held themselves as if they had been trained in war. Most looked miserable and awkward and would be more likely to hurt *themselves* with swords and bows in their hands than anyone else.

'They aren't soldiers,' whispered Lena to Sir Poland. 'What's going on?'

'I know,' Sir Poland replied just as quietly. 'Keep your eyes open and we'll talk of it later.'

Up through the Keep Lena and Sir Poland went, up through the winding stairwells and past the arrow-slits that lined the walls until they finally reached a room at the top. Lena guessed it was the Duke's audience chamber. They entered and inside Lena saw a man who must be the Duke standing with a small group of guards.

Duke Winlow was a thin, pale man. He looked tired and old and his weak arms could barely hold the sword in his hand. However, upon seeing the sword, Lena and Sir Poland drew their own. It could be a trap thought Lena, you never knew.

'Put your weapons down,' said the Duke. 'Please. I won't attack you.'

'I command you in the name of the King, to surrender,' said Sir Poland. There was iron and rage in his voice.

'We'll do this properly,' said the Duke. He bent down onto one knee and placed his sword on the floor. 'The King has won, Sir Knight. I hope you're proud, but at least I have your attention. That is something.'

This was all wrong, Lena thought to herself. The Order was expecting a proper fight, but it looked like it was over with barely a sword swung.

One of the Duke's guards suddenly turned to address the Duke. 'My lord, is this-?'

'It's over, James,' replied Duke Winlow. He pointed at Sir Poland. 'That is a knight of the Order of the Furnace. Feel free to fight him if you like but you'll be throwing your life away.'

He then turned to Sir Poland. 'I had hoped you were all still in the North. I knew there was no hope of success, but I thought if we were fighting the King's army then we could hold them off for a time at least.'

'The Northern War ended sooner than we thought,' Sir Poland replied. 'We won.'

'That's a shame,' the Duke replied. 'We knew you had to return eventually, but by then I thought our movement would have progressed further. We prayed you might even join us.'

Sir Poland raised his hands and took off his helmet. It hissed as the seals broke. 'Duke Winlow, I don't understand. What in blazes is going on? To rebel against your King is a terrible crime.'

'You really have no idea do you?' said the Duke. 'Things have changed in the empire while you've been away, Sir Knight. I've been trying to speak to your Grand Master for months but I am guessing none of my messages have reached you.'

'He has told me nothing,' said Sir Poland.

'King Claudio is sucking the kingdom dry, my lord. His endless wars building his empire are slowly killing us. We give him our food, our clothes, our sons and daughters, and he just takes and takes, more and more. It never ends. He's killing us and we had to do something.'

'So you rebelled?' asked Lena. Sir Poland looked at her sternly. 'Sorry.'

'Some other dukes and I banded together and told the King to stop, but he didn't listen and instead branded us traitors. Duke Stonewall and Duke Ignacio are under siege as we speak, and I've heard Dukes Regatta and Emerson are dead already, at the hands of the Jasareen most likely.'

'I haven't heard any of this,' said Sir Poland.

'I expect the King thought you didn't need to know,' said Duke Winlow. 'One or two dukes rebelling can be put down to madness, five will make people wonder-'

Before the Duke could continue there was a crash of door being flung open. Lena spun around and saw Erin walk into the audience chamber with her soldiers behind her.

'Duke Winlow, stop talking at once,' Erin ordered.

'You are under arrest as a traitor to the crown and will be questioned in Casenberg. Any further words spoken here will be seen as evidence of your crimes against the King .'

'Let the Duke finish,' said Sir Poland angrily. 'I want to know what's going on.'

Erin looked at Sir Poland. 'It's not your place to question prisoners, knight. You've done your duty admirably today and the King thanks you, but now it's my turn. Leave this to your betters.'

Lena winced at Erin's last remark and she saw her master tense.

'*Betters?* Be careful, Grand Minister-' growled Sir Poland.

'Be silent,' said Erin, her voice cold. She stepped forward and raised a finger. 'I speak with the authority of the King himself. Do not try my patience or I'll have you sent to Casenberg too. Have you forgotten your vows like the Duke here? Did the Northern War knock them from your memory?'

The huge knight said no more, but Lena dared not even breathe in case Sir Poland exploded. She had never seen him so furious.

Erin turned to her soldiers. 'Take the Duke away. If he says one more word, cut him down before he can say a second.'

Two of Erin's soldiers went to the Duke, took his arms, and led him out of his audience chamber. The Duke looked miserable but didn't resist. Erin followed them out.

Sir Poland watched Erin leave and then, without warning, punched the stone wall nearby. He walked off, leaving Lena alone with the Duke's men. They looked at her fearfully but said nothing.

# Chapter Nine

Grandmaster Alberto, ruler of the Order of the Furnace, sat at the high table at the far end of the Twisted Keep's Great Hall, the home of the Order. It was now late at night and the summer sun had retreated behind the mountains to the East. The Great Hall was awash with torchlight.

It had been two months since the siege of Castle Winlow and rumour had it things in the Empire were turning sour. Dark thoughts weighed heavily on the Grandmaster's mind. He had served the Order of the Furnace his entire life and for the first time ever he was uncertain of its future.

Standing opposite the Grandmaster was Sir Poland. Sir Poland stood at attention.

'So what have we learned?' asked Grandmaster Alberto, his chin resting on his knuckles. He sounded very tired.

'Things are much worse than we thought, my lord,' Sir Poland replied.

'Go on.'

'The King has replaced a large number of the dukes and counts in the kingdom with those more loyal to him,' said Sir Poland. 'Duke Winlow was just one of many. Most barely put up any sort of fight. Those like Winlow who fought back have all been placed in the dungeons of Casenberg.'

Grandmaster Alberto stared at the water-filled goblet in his hand, took a sip then looked at Sir Poland. 'So what do you advise?'

'I think the King will come for us but I cannot be certain,' Sir Poland replied

'It would be a great risk.'

'Of course, but the King has over a hundred thousand soldiers under arms. They would win eventually.'

'So what do you suggest we do?' asked the Grandmaster.

'I've made plans,' replied Sir Poland. 'But we cannot be seen to make the first move.'

'I agree,' said the Grandmaster. 'Have you spoken to Madeleine?'

'She's been warned,' said Sir Poland. 'However, there are problems.'

'Such as?'

'Oliguer isn't working.'

The Grandmaster looked startled. 'What? Why not?'

'Madeleine isn't sure. He's been asleep for a long time. She's looking into it'

'Good,' said Grandmaster Alberto. 'This could get very ugly, Alberghast. We'll need Oliguer if we have any hope of surviving.'

'I know, my lord.'

'You're dismissed, Sir Knight,' said Grandmaster Alberto. He sat back in his high-backed chair and Sir Poland turned and marched out of the Great hall.

Once outside, Sir Poland walked across the courtyard to the Knight's cloister. He went inside and to his cell where he sat at his desk and composed a letter.

*Dear Nestor...* it began.

Once he was finished he stepped outside and caught one of the Order attendants who was walking by. He handed the letter to the attendant and ordered him to see it was delivered. The attendant nodded his head and left.

Sir Poland watched him go and prayed the message would get through. Things were about to get very bad, he thought to himself. He could feel it in his bones.

# Chapter Ten

The afternoon sunlight glinted off blunted swords as they flew through the air.

*Swish! Swish! Clang! Swish!*

Lena and Berry stood fighting in the middle of a training ring in the courtyard of the Twisted Keep. Around them stood the other squires cheering the girls on while Kruger watched them with his arms folded in front of him.

Lena and Berry moved like dancers to avoid each other's blows, their blades slicing the air where their limbs had been only moments before. It was almost hypnotic.

Seeing an opportunity, Lena twisted her weapon and stabbed at Berry, but Berry arched to the right and Lena's blade passed under her armpit. Berry then brought her own sword around towards Lena's head and Lena jumped back just in time.

'You need to do better than that!' Berry called out.

She ran at Lena and their swords crashed together once again.

Suddenly, Berry swung hard and Lena parried awkwardly. Seeing her advantage, Berry moved into a better position and pushed Lena back.

Lena tried to get out of Berry's way but Berry wouldn't let her. She took a step backwards, lost her footing, and tumbled to the ground. No sooner had she fallen than Berry's sword was at her throat.

'Got you!' cried Berry triumphantly.

Lena slapped the ground in frustration. 'Lucky,' she spat.

'Yield?' Berry asked.

'I yield,' said Lena, her eyes like daggers.

Berry gave Lena a quick jab in the stomach.

'Ow!' shouted Lena. I said I yield!'

'I know,' Berry replied. 'That was for the way you looked at me. It wasn't nice.'

'You deserved it,' said Lena. 'Stop showing off.'

Berry smiled. 'You're going to have a nasty mark. Want another?'

'Enough,' called out Kruger. Well done, Berry.'

He turned to the rest of the class 'So,' he continued. 'Where did Lena go wrong?'

'She fought Berry?' said Ton Singh. The rest of the class laughed.

Kruger waited for the laughing to die down.

'Twenty circuits of the courtyard, Singh.' He then looked at the rest of the class. 'Anyone else want to be a joker? No? Good. Serious answers please.'

For the next five minutes Lena sat in the dust listening to her friends and classmates suggest reasons why she had lost. It wasn't fun.

'You're all partly right,' said Kruger. He explained what Lena had done wrong and when he finished he turned and looked at Lena. 'So you won't be making that mistake again will you? Stand up.'

Berry offered her hand to Lena and Lena took it.

Once on her feet, Lena tried to give Berry a quick shove with her shoulder while Kruger wasn't looking, but Berry moved away, leaving Lena unbalanced.

Berry then used her leg to take Lena's out from under her. She fell to the ground again with a bump.

'Nice try,' hissed Berry. Lena growled at her.

Kruger looked at both of them, rolled his eyes, and turned back the other squires. 'Right, who's next?'

Silas and Michael Obasi raised their hands and stepped

forward, but before they could begin a trumpet-call echoed across the Twisted Keep's courtyard.

Someone was coming.

Lena looked towards the gate house. She watched the Order's guards take hold of the great metal rings on each door and pull the gate open. Through the gates rode a small group of people. Lena could see a dark banner with a wolf's head fluttering in the breeze and soldiers on horses.

The person at the front of the column was Erin. The Grand Minister rode to the Keep's entrance, dismounted and strode inside. Her soldiers followed her.

'We'll stop for fifteen minutes,' said Kruger. He looked concerned. 'Put your weapons away and get something to drink. I'll be back soon.' Kruger turned and made his way towards the Keep as Erin and the other riders went inside, leaving the squires to tidy up after themselves.

Lena put her sword back on the rack and looked at her friends. 'Want to see what Erin wants?' she asked. Berry, Silas, and the rest nodded in unison as Ton Singh came back, out of breath.

'I do too!' huffed Ton.

The squires left the courtyard, entered the Twisted Keep and made their way through its kitchens and narrow passageways.

The Twisted Keep itself was one of the last remains of the Old Wars and had been warped and bent by monstrous forces hundreds of years ago; corridors would curl away and turn into sheer drops and many rooms had floors that would become walls as you walked through them. The squires had lived there for years and knew the place like the back of their hands.

Soon enough they arrived at the gallery above the Great Hall. Below they could hear an argument.

# Chapter Eleven

In the gallery above the Great Hall, the squires got to their knees and sneaked over to the railing where they could hide while still being able to listen to what was going on below.

Lena looked down and saw a few knights gathered around the top table, including Grandmaster Alberto and Seneschal Maglan, second in command of the Order. In front of the knights was Grand Minister Erin. She stood with her soldiers and her arms were crossed. Lena couldn't help but notice the soldiers were armed: crossbows were held loosely in their arms.

Grandmaster Alberto sat in the middle of the head-table and Seneschal Maglan stood next to him, her eyes locked on Erin and her hand clamped to her great-sword. Occasionally she would bend down and whisper into the Grandmaster's ear and the Grandmaster would furrow his brow.

The squires listened as Erin spoke.

'...and the King requests you hand over all your weapons and armaments, placing them under royal command immediately,' said Erin. 'The Order of the Furnace will become a Royal Order and no longer independent.'

The knights and the squires all gasped as one. Lena threw her hand over her mouth and looked at the other squires wide-eyed. Thankfully the ruckus in the Great Hall masked the sound.

'You must understand, Grandmaster,' continued Erin. 'The world has changed and your Order needs to change with it. The King requests you submit immediately.'

'How *dare* you, Erin,' fumed the Grandmaster, smashing his flagon down on the table. 'The Order has served the kingdom faithfully for hundreds of years! We will not lay down arms just for Claudio's ambitions!'

Erin looked angry. 'Do not speak of your King so incautiously, my lord. Your Order's gifts could be better used by the King without having to follow your silly rules.'

'So that's it,' snorted the Grandmaster. 'Since the siege at Castle Winlow we have guessed as much and have been waiting for this day, even though we hoped it would never come. Get out, Erin! I will not have the Order become some cruel tool for a power-mad despot.' The Grandmaster stood up. 'I, Grandmaster Alberto de Lorenzo, formally cease the Order's relationship with the kingdom and Empire of Eltsvine. The Twisted Keep, its vassals no longer answer to King Claudio!'

The room filled with grunts and gasps. Lena felt the temperature drop a few degrees.

Erin smiled. 'Then I accuse the Order of the Furnace of treason. I command you to lay down your weapons and accompany me to Casenberg to await trial. You're a relic, Alberto, and you'll be first thrown in Casenberg's dungeons and then onto the scrap pile.'

'We will see you on the battlefield,' said the Grandmaster. 'Get out.'

Erin stayed where she was and smiled. 'I don't think so.'

Lady Maglan stepped forward. 'Leave if you know what's good for you, Erin.' She drew her sword. 'No one speaks to the Grandmaster that way.'

Erin raised her hand and her soldiers raised their crossbows. The room held its breath.

'What do you think you are doing?' said the Grandmaster. 'You hope to fight us here? In our home? With only a few soldiers?'

'Alberto,' said Erin. 'Tell your knights to lay down their arms. You *will* come with us. This is your last warning.'

'You're mad, Erin. Utterly mad,' said the Grandmaster.

Lady Maglan took another step forward. There was a *whoosh*, a cry, and Lena watched as Lady Maglan fell to the floor with a cross-bow bolt in her side.

'Eliza, no!' cried the Grandmaster. He bounded forward and put his hand on Lady Maglan's side; when he lifted it again there was blood.

'I will *kill* you, Erin!' the Grandmaster snarled. He got up and he and the other knights drew their swords. They charged.

Erin's soldiers were ready for them. They fired crossbows and knights fell. Those that didn't smashed into the royal soldiers and the fighting began in earnest.

Up in the gallery the squires looked on, horrified. It was chaos down there.

'This can't be happening...' said Silas.

'We need to get down there!' cried Berry.

Moments later, a voice from below called to them. It was Kruger. 'Get to the cloister!' he shouted, waving the squires away before attacking the soldier nearest to him. 'Get to your masters! Tell them what has happened!'

Lena looked down at Kruger and nodded. She and the other squires then turned and ran out of the gallery. They moved quickly, back through the Keep's hidden passages and past frantic servants who had heard about the events in the Great Hall.

The squires ran through the kitchens and out into the darkening courtyard. Once there they skidded to a stop.

'Oh, no!' cried Ton.

Across the courtyard, the squires saw the gate house open once again. Royal soldiers poured in; hundreds of them in full armour, ready for battle. Order knights and soldiers ran to push them back but it was clear they were going to be overrun very soon.

'Where did they come from?' asked Silas.

'This was all planned,' said Lena.

'How do you know that?' asked Berry, who had never paid much attention to strategy lessons.

'It's the only thing that makes sense,' Lena replied. 'Erin knew the Grandmaster would refuse her. She must have put an army in Upsalom last night.'

'But our families are in Upsalom!' said Michael Obasi.

'Look!' cried Silas.

Lena looked to where Silas was pointing. On the roof of the gate house were cloaked figures moving like ghosts.

'Jasareen!' said Lena. 'They must have opened the gates!'

Berry, rather than turning to the cloister as they had been commanded, suddenly ran over to the training racks, grabbed a sword and headed towards the gate house.

'What are you doing?' cried Lena.

'Helping!' Berry called back. She then ran across to the royal soldiers and started swinging. The two royal soldiers closest to Berry fell.

'Wait here,' said Lena to the other squires. She ran after Berry, dodging thrusting swords and spears until she reached her friend.

'We can't do this!' Lena called out, ducking as a halberd swept the air above her. She kicked out and the soldier fell to the ground with a grunt. 'There are too many! You'll just get yourself killed!'

Berry ignored Lena. Instead, she continued swinging like she would never tire. Lena got even closer; narrowly avoiding being hit by Berry.

'Come on, you heard Kruger!'

Berry turned and looked at Lena. 'But-'

Lena grabbed her friend by the shoulder. 'We can't stay here. We just we can't.'

Berry and Lena edged backwards, letting the Order's guards take their places.

Ok, I'm with you,' said Berry, breathless now but calmer.

'As soon as we find Sir Poland we'll come straight back here,' said Lena. 'I promise.'

# Chapter Twelve

The squires swiftly made their way to the cloister. When they arrived, the cloister was a hive of activity. News must have already reached them about the attack.

'Get inside!' said Lena.

The squires entered and found people running everywhere. Lena led the squires through the cloister until they reached the stairwell that would lead them to their masters' living quarters upstairs.

As Lena's foot touched the first step, there was a shattering of glass. Nearby, a window fell inwards in pieces. Glass scattered over the ground as a black figure burst through. The figure landed on her feet and looked at the squires. Her face was covered in a black metal mask and in each hand was a long knife.

It was a Jasareen assassin.

Lena and Berry moved to the front of the squires and pushed their friends behind them. 'Run!' said Lena, and the squires bolted up the stairwell.

The assassin looked at Berry and Lena curiously. Her eyes flicked between the squires, and Lena guessed she was trying to work out which of them was the easier target.

The assassin lunged at Lena, knives aimed at her throat and heart. Lena dodged and Berry used her blunted sword to knock the knives from their path. The assassin moved past the squires, spun around and stood on the stairwell.

'Forty-four?' asked Berry from the corner of her mouth.

Lena nodded.

Berry surged forward, her sword coming down in an

attempt to break the assassin's leg. As the assassin anticipated the attack and moved, Lena swept to Berry's right, put her hand on Berry's shoulder and jumped forward with her feet in front of her. Lena's feet hit the assassin in the shoulder and the assassin staggered back, but the assassin also brought her knife upwards. Lena twisted in the air and felt the knife cut skin.

Meanwhile, Berry made her next move. She pushed her sword forward, aiming for the Jasareen's side. The sword hit the assassin in the ribs but the sword was blunt. What should have been a fatal blow must only have broken one of the assassin's ribs. Lena noticed the assassin didn't make a noise even when their rib snapped.

Lena knew most opponents would have run away at this point, but the assassin did something highly unexpected. The assassin turned, ran up a few steps, crouched, and then pushed themselves into the air. Lena and Berry watched as the Jasareen flew over their heads. They ducked just in time as the assassin's blades swept downwards. The girls nearly fell over each other trying to stay alive.

'That was impressive!' gasped Berry.

When the assassin landed, she didn't give the squires a moment to recover. She lunged again.

Berry quickly crouched, letting one of the knives sweep above her; then she stood up, and started to swing her sword, but instead of finishing she brought her fist into the assassin's stomach in a surprise move.

'Argh!' Berry cried. Her fist had hit metal. Underneath the assassin's clothes there must have been layers of armour. Berry crumpled to the ground, wrapping her body around her injured hand.

'Berry!' cried Lena.

As the assassin moved past, Lena moved to stand over her friend, shielding her.

The assassin looked at the two girls and Lena thought she could feel her smiling. There was no way Lena could fight a Jasareen on her own. All Lena could do was run and that would mean leaving Berry.

Then Lena saw something and smiled.

The assassin was about to move forward for the killing blow when they paused. She looked down and saw an armoured fist on her arm. Turning, the assassin was suddenly hit by Lady Openden's other fist. Her mask crumpled and she slid to the floor with a grunt.

Lady Openden then picked up the assassin and threw her out of the broken window.

'Thank you!' said Lena.

Lady Openden nodded. 'Go. I'll take it from here.'

Lena helped Berry up and they flew up the stairwell. At the top they found the other squires; Sir Poland was standing over them.

'Lena?' said Sir Poland. 'Where have you been? What's going on?'

'Kruger wants you to come to the great hall, Milord!' said Lena. 'Erin attacked the grandmaster! Lady Maglan's hurt and royal soldiers are pouring into the Keep too!'

Sir Poland looked at Lena and paused. 'So it's happened. This way.'

Lena looked at Sir Poland with a puzzled expression. 'Shouldn't we be going back to the hall?'

There was a noise downstairs. More royal soldiers were coming.

Sir Poland turned and commanded some knights nearby to stop the enemy entering the cloister. Then he turned to Lena and the other squires once again. 'Not yet. Come with me.'

Lena and the other squires followed Sir Poland through the cloister. At the far end of the long corridor that ran the length of the first floor they came to the storeroom where blankets, candles and other bits and pieces for the knights' cells were kept.

Sir Poland opened the door, moved a box and uncovered the trapdoor underneath. He opened it and gestured for the squires to jump down. They did so and Sir Poland followed them.

Lena and the squires found themselves in the cloister kitchens.

Sir Poland ran to the kitchen door, turned the key, and then slid the bolts across. 'That should give us enough time,' he said.

While Sir Poland locked the door, Lena quickly patched up Berry's hand. It looked red and sore, and Berry had lost some skin on her knuckles, but at least it wasn't broken.

'You must get away,' said Sir Poland. He looked over the squires. 'All of you listen! Go to Swanslight copse, just outside of town. You should be safely out the way while the fighting goes on. If the Keep falls-'

'Don't say that!' cried Lena.

*'If the Keep falls*, I need you to go to the village of Ivanmoon and find a man called Nestor. Tell him what has happened. He will know what to do. Do you know the place?'

Lena nodded. 'I remember it from your maps.'

Sir Poland reached up to his armour and took Pandora's medallion.

'This is for you, Lena. I want you to take Pandora with you. With any luck, you'll bring her back to me soon.'

Lena trembled. 'No-'

'You *will* take her Lena and lead the squires to Nestor if need be. Keep her covered and look after her. I want to see her again.'

Sir Poland then turned back to the other squires. 'You will listen to Lena and do as she says; she speaks for me from now on until I command otherwise. I hope to see you all very soon but, if not, you follow her no matter what. Do you understand me?'

Most of the squires were too shocked by what was happening to answer properly; they just nodded dumbly.

Sir Poland moved to the other end of the kitchen, away from the door that was now being hammered upon from outside. He reached up to the mantle-piece above the main fire and pressed something. There was a *click* and a section of the kitchen wall rolled back.

The hammering at the door got louder. Wood was cracking.

'Go, quickly,' said Sir Poland. 'Follow the passageway. It'll lead you out of the Twisted Keep and into the stables. Find Pandora and tell her what's happened. She'll understand. Good luck.'

'What about you?' asked Lena.

'We'll see,' said Sir Poland. 'Go!'

Lena and the other Squires barrelled into the secret passageway. Once everyone was through Lena turned back to see the opening to the kitchen shut again. She pressed her ear to it. Beyond, she heard the kitchen door finally break then the sound of swords clashing.

'He'll be fine,' said Berry.

'I hope so,' Lena replied.

# Chapter Thirteen

In the hidden passageway the squires found torches on the walls. Using the flint and tinder they kept with them at all times they lit the torches and then moved swiftly down the dim passageway, away from the fighting. Soon enough, they came to a dead-end with a switch set into the wall. Lena flicked the switch and the wall swung away.

Lena leaned out of the secret passageway and saw they were at the Order's stables.

'It's clear,' she said to the others. 'Let's go.'

The squires came out of the passageway and fanned out into the stables. The horses snorted at the sight of them while the Archons stood completely still. Against the far wall were swords, armour, bedding and other items they might need; as if this escape had been expected.

Lena pointed at the equipment and the horses. 'Get what you need,' she ordered. The squires nodded and did what they were told as quickly as they could without making too much noise.

While the squires went to the stalls and harnessed their horses, Lena grabbed a travel pack and sword and went to Pandora.

Pandora stood tall, majestic and motionless in her stall. Lena took the medallion Sir Poland had given her, placed it in the depression on Pandora's neck and took it away again. Pandora came to life; swishing her head and looking at Lena with her glowing, glassy eyes.

Lena explained what had happened in the Twisted Keep. She felt silly talking to an Archon but she had seen Sir Poland do it before and after each battle so she guessed it must mean something. Lena wasn't sure if Pandora understood but the Archon lowered her head as if to say she did.

'We need to go to Swanslight copse. Do you know the way?'

Pandora nodded slowly again.

Lena went to Pandora's side, reached up and pulled herself onto the saddle. It felt very strange being there - like she was an imposter. This was Sir Poland's mount not hers. She turned to look at the other knights and squires. They were looking at her differently too.

'She suits you,' said Berry quietly.

'Let's go,' Lena said grimly. 'And be careful.'

Lena and the other squires cantered out of the stables and, once outside, looked up towards the Twisted Keep. The sun was going down and the Keep was now outlined against the sky. Fire-orange flickered in the dusk and cries carried on the wind.

Lena felt a hole in her heart. What would happen now? Even if Sir Poland and the others managed to push the Royal Army back that wouldn't be the end of it. King Claudio and Grand Minister Erin would hardly give up. Lena understood what had been her life for many years was being destroyed, regardless of whether the Order won or lost. Things would not be back to normal for a very long time. However, it did look like Sir Poland had a plan. She hoped above all else that it would work and she'd be back in the Twisted Keep before too long.

Lena geed Pandora and led the other squires down a path that would pass the edge of Upsalom, the town that sat in the shadow of the Twisted Keep.

# Chapter Fourteen

The castle town of Upsalom was silent when the young knights arrived. Nothing moved and no lights were on. Occasionally something would creak and leaves would rustle, but little else made a sound. The town should have been full of people who were all associated with the Order in some way: families of knights and squires lived here, along with the servants, cooks, guards and gardeners who looked after the Twisted Keep.

'We need to check things out,' said Lena.

The squires dismounted, tied up their horses and crept closer to the houses.

'Where is everyone?' asked Silas quietly.

'Erin must have them hiding somewhere,' replied Lena.

Suddenly there was the sound on footsteps on cobbles nearby.

'Hide!' hissed Lena.

The knights jumped and hid in the shadow of a low wall. They peeked over the top and from one street saw two soldiers in royal armour. The soldiers marched past the squires and entered one of the town's buildings.

'They must have taken over the town,' said Lena.

'What should we do?' asked Gregory DeLure.

'Follow orders,' said Lena. 'Let's get to Swanslight copse. We can't do much here anyway.'

'Lena, I need to make sure my family is okay,' said Berry. Some other the other squires agreed. 'We'll be quick.' Berry started to leave.

'No!' hissed Lena.

Berry turned and looked at Lena in surprise. 'But-!'

'It's too dangerous,' said Lena. 'I'm sorry, Berry.'

Berry looked as if she was about to argue but then thought better of it and nodded. 'Okay.'

Lena led the young knights back to their mounts. 'We'll have to loop around to the copse in case there are more soldiers,' she said. 'Follow me.'

The squires followed Lena and kept themselves out of the way of Upsalom, going through fields and crossing brooks until they reached Swanslight copse. Lena noticed that Berry kept looking back over her shoulder.

Swanslight copse was a small cluster of trees half a mile or so from Upsalom. If someone stood in the middle of it they would be hidden from anyone passing by. Also, it was far enough away from Upsalom that it would be unlikely any soldiers would be looking there anyway. The squires would be safe for the time being. Sir Poland had picked a good spot.

The squires arrived in the copse and started to dismount in silence.

'Ton,' said Lena. 'Go to the Keep and see what's happening. We'll wait an hour for you and if you're not back by then, we'll head to Ivanmoon. You can catch up with us there.'

Ton nodded and slid off his horse. 'Sure,' he replied. 'Back soon.' He then disappeared into the darkness, heading towards the glowing Keep.

The others tied up their horses and sat around, huddling next to one another for warmth and comfort. The minutes dragged by slowly and every noise nearby made them jump despite their training. They didn't speak to one another, fearing they might be heard or their words might bring sobs they wouldn't be able to hold back.

Later, there was a rustle nearby. The squires stood and drew their swords as one but thankfully only Ton appeared.

'What's going on?' asked Lena.

Ton looked at Lena darkly.

'The Grand Minister has everyone,' he said. 'I hid near the drawbridge and watched. I saw Lord Alberto and Sir Poland leave the Keep in chains along with the others. All the other squires were caught too.'

'What happened then?'

'They were put onto wagons.' Ton then pulled out a piece of paper. 'Erin had these stuck to the Keep's walls.'

Lena took the paper and read it before passing it on to Berry and the others.

*"Do not enter. Property of the King,"* it read.

'What happened to the Royal Army?' asked Lena.

'They're all leaving,' Ton replied. 'It looked like they were going to Casenberg.'

'Lena-' started Berry. 'Our families. If Erin has gone... Please.'

'Do it,' said Lena. She looked at the young knights. 'But if you're not back here in an hour then you'll have to make your way to Ivanmoon on your own. Understand? It's too dangerous to wait or look for you.'

The squires nodded and split up, vanishing in to the night. The copse was now empty except for Lena and Silas.

'Can I come with you?' asked Silas. 'I'd rather not stay here on my own.'

'Sure,' said Lena. 'Come on.'

# Chapter Fifteen

Lena and Silas sat on their mounts and trotted along one of the roadways that led from Upsalom to Lena's parents' farm. The moon shone in the sky, insects buzzed in the fields and in the hedgerows either side of the road, and occasionally they caught a glimpse of an animal's eyes shining out from a thicket.

At first they rode in silence, but after a time Lena could see Silas wanted to say something.

'We're not going to be going back to the Twisted Keep for a while are we?' asked Silas glumly.

'No,' Lena replied. 'Not for a while.'

'What's going to happen in Ivanmoon?'

'I've no idea,' said Lena. 'We need to find this Nestor first. We'll figure it out from there.'

'That's not much of a plan,' muttered Silas.

'I know, but there's not much else we can do. We're hardly going to storm Casenberg on our own are we?'

When they got closer to Lena's parents' farm they saw two more horses with the royal livery on them.

'Oh, no!' gasped Lena. 'What are they doing here?'

They dismounted and Silas tied his horse to Pandora. The squires then tiptoed towards the front of the farmhouse. There, they hopped over a low stone wall and sneaked up to one of the windows.

When they peered through they saw the two royal soldiers speaking with Lena's parents, who looked both worried and furious at the same time.

'You're to come with us,' said one of the Soldiers, gruffly.

'By order of the King.'

'We've done nothing wrong!' said Lena's father. 'You can't do this. You've kept us here all night and now you want to take us away?'

'Your daughter was a squire in the Order of the Furnace, sir.'

'What are you saying?'

'They are traitors now. And you might be traitors too. We have to bring everyone in.'

'Traitors? Ridiculous! Where's Lena?' shouted Lena's mother. 'What have you done with her?'

'I don't know, ma'am,' said the soldier who seemed to be the more senior of the two. 'There was a lot of fighting at the Keep...'

Lena's mother slumped and Lena's father grabbed her.

'Get out!' cried Lena's mother, rising suddenly and swinging at the soldier.

'There were prisoners,' the soldier continued, not unkindly. 'She might still be alive...'

'Might?' screamed Lena's mother. '*Might?!*'

'This is going to turn ugly,' said Lena quietly. 'We should-', she turned to Silas but her friend had gone. 'Silas!' Lena hissed, looking around. 'Where are you?'

Lena peered through the window once again and saw the back door to the farmhouse open slowly. Silas crept into the kitchen, moving like a cat. Neither the soldiers nor Lena's parent's knew he was there.

Lena could only watch as Silas attacked. The first soldier was down without so much as a cry and the second collapsed before he had a chance to react. Both soldiers now lay on the floor, unconscious.

'Who are *you*?' Lena heard her mother. 'Get out! Get out!'

Lena burst through the front door. 'He's with me, mum! It's me Lena!'

'Lena? Lena!' her parents cried.

'They didn't hurt you did they?' Lena asked frantically. She rushed over to her mother and put her arms around her. She looked at her father.

'Thank the Gods you're alive!' said Lena's father. 'We were so worried!' He pulled out a chair from under the kitchen table and helped Lena's mother sit down. 'What's going on? These men said the Order were now traitors.'

'The King has gone mad,' Lena replied. 'He attacked us but we managed to escape.'

'Where are the other knights?' asked Lena's father.

'The Twisted Keep has been overrun. We think they have been taken to Casenberg.'

Lena saw Silas trying to get her attention and followed his eyes to the soldiers on the floor. Silas then looked at the two men and then the back door. Lena nodded. 'Do it,' she ordered. Lena then turned back to her parents while Silas dragged the first soldier out back.

'What will you do?' asked Lena's parents as Silas returned and dragged the second soldier outside.

'We have orders,' said Lena. Her parents didn't question her further. They knew she couldn't tell them what she had been told to do.

'Who's he?' asked Lena's mother, looking at Silas, who had returned and stood quietly at the kitchen door.

'He's another squire. Silas, this is my mum and dad. Mum and dad, this is Silas.' Lena replied.

'Hi,' said Silas.

'Only you two escaped?' asked Lena's father.

'No, there are others,' Lena replied. 'They're checking up on their families.'

'Can't you stay here until all this blows over?' wondered Lena mother.

'No, it's too dangerous, mum. The King will work out

we're missing soon enough and he'll come looking.' Lena could see her parents understood what this meant for them. 'I'm sorry. You should hide too. Can you stay with anyone?'

'The Listers in Topper-yarn would put us up,' said Lena's father. 'They've been wanting us to visit anyway. They're trustworthy too and won't say anything.'

'Good, but don't tell them any more than you have to.'

'Well I suppose that's it,' said Lena's mother. 'We need to get a few things.'

Lena's parents hugged their daughter again and left the kitchen. They started collecting all the valuables they could carry from around the house while Lena and Silas sat at the kitchen table.

'Where are the soldiers?' asked Lena. 'Did you...?'

'No. They're tied up in the barn. The ropes should hold them while we get away.'

'Thanks. And thanks for earlier.'

'It's okay,' said Silas.

Soon enough, Lena's parents had collected their things. They gathered outside and Lena and Silas helped Lena's parents load their cart for the coming journey.

'Be safe, Lena,' said Lena's mother, once they were finished. 'And good luck.'

'You too,' Lena replied.

Lena hugged her parents. They climbed onto the cart, said their final goodbyes and left their farm. Lena and Silas watched them go until they vanished over a low hill.

'When do you think you'll see them again?' asked Silas, watching the cart disappear around a bend.

'I don't know,' Lena replied. 'Soon I hope. Let's get back.'

Lena and Silas left the farm, found Pandora and Silas' horse, and went back to Swanslight copse. They rode back in silence.

When they arrived, the other squires had already returned.

Lena heard crying and saw Samir, Lizzy and Elsa looking very unhappy.

'What happened?' asked Lena to Berry.

'Their parents weren't in their homes,' explained Berry. 'It looked like there had been fighting.'

Berry had her arm around Lizzy's shoulders. 'We think they might have been taken.'

Lena nodded then spoke to the others.

'We need to get to Ivanmoon as soon as we can. We can't stay here. Maybe there we can do something about all this. Our friends and family have been taken but we won't give up. Sir Poland has a plan and we will fight back.'

No one argued but Lena felt she hadn't convinced them. They could see what was going on as well as she could: the future looked bleak.

The squires got on their horses and rode out of town, away from their old lives.

# Chapter Sixteen

Sir Poland sat in one of the Royal Army wagons and he couldn't see a thing. At the Keep, Erin's soldiers had tied his and the other knights' hands behind their backs and thrown sacks over their heads so they couldn't see, then they were bundled into these wagons without a word.

Around him he could feel the presence of others.

'Who's here?' Sir Poland whispered.

Five other knights answered back in hushed tones: Sir Ferhal, Lady Yelinka, Lady Hawthorne, Lady Isiti and, Sir Litten.

'Sir Poland?' hissed Lady Yelinka. 'Is that you?'

'It is,' replied Sir Poland. 'I am glad to hear you are all well.'

'What will happen to us?' asked Sir Litten.

'I know not,' said Sir Poland. 'But have faith.'

As they rumbled on to Casenberg, Sir Poland prayed to every God he could think of that Lena and the other squires would reach Nestor before it was too late. If they could reach Nestor and then Madeleine they might have a chance...

Suddenly, the wagon came to a stop. Sir Poland could hear the door being flung open angrily.

'Where are they?' screeched Erin. 'Your squires! Where are they? *Tell me!!*'

Sir Poland just smiled.

# Chapter Seventeen

It took a week and a half to reach the outskirts of Ivanmoon. The squires had kept off the main roads, made camp far away from prying eyes, and lived off the land. Thankfully, they were excellent hunters; they didn't go hungry.

The journey had been uneventful. The squires, all well trained, kept to acting and behaving as if they were on a march. Lena didn't want them to think about what had happened at the Twisted Keep too much, so she had assigned tasks to everyone and had them training in the evening. It looked like it had worked at the end of the week; the squires seemed to be in better moods than at the start of their journey.

During the middle of the second week of riding, the squires found themselves making their way into a valley where Lena knew they would find Ivanmoon. The squires took their horses down the slope of the valley, all the way to the bottom; mindful of loose rocks and hidden falls.

Eventually they reached the pine forest that covered the valley floor. Above the tree-line they could see smoke from chimneys rising to the sky. They entered the forest and when they were closer to the village Lena raised her hand and called for the squires to stop.

'Berry, Silas,' said Lena. 'Let's find this Nestor. The rest of you wait here.' She pointed at a stream that flowed nearby. 'Water your horses and eat. We'll be back soon.'

Lena and her two companions made their way through the gloomy forest. It was dense and ominous, like something out of a fairy tale. The trees loomed over them. Occasionally, a lone bird would call out, but nothing else stirred.

'How are we going to find Nestor?' asked Berry.

'We can ask around, I suppose,' said Lena. She looked into the distance. The roofs of Ivanmoon could now be seen clearly through the trees. 'Ivanmoon doesn't look that big. It shouldn't be hard to find him.'

The trees stopped and buildings appeared. Ivanmoon was a barren, desolate place just like the forest that surrounded it and the squires saw very few villagers wandering the streets. Whenever they did see someone, they tried to approach them but the villager would hurry away.

'What's wrong with everyone?' asked Silas.

'This is useless,' said Berry. 'I'm just going to grab the next person and ask them where Nestor is, whether they like it or not.'

The squires turned a corner and came to the village square. At the far end of the square was a large building with columns that must be the village hall and in the middle of the square was an old fountain. Near the fountain the squires saw a few boys pushing each other around and laughing; it was a strange sound in this place.

'How about asking them?' asked Berry.

Lena looked the boys over. 'They'll have to do,' she answered grimly. They didn't look particularly friendly but the squires went over to the boys anyway. They didn't have many other options.

'What do we have here-' started the biggest boy, but Berry didn't give him a chance to finish. She punched the closest boy on the chin, knocked the second off his feet with a kick and, as quick as a snake, grabbed the biggest boy by his dirty shirt and brought a knife to his throat.

'Berry!' cried Lena.

'Grh'ak!' said the boy, terrified. 'Snar'glk!!'

Berry glanced at Lena. 'This saves time.'

'Sorry about her,' said Lena stepping up next to Berry.

'We'll be quick. Do you know a man called Nestor?'

'H'ak?' replied the boy, trying not to move his neck in any way. The other two boys were shuffling on the floor, backing away in fear.

'Berry, I think you're distracting him,' said Lena.

Berry withdrew the knife and slipped in back into its scabbard. The boy's eyes never left it.

'We're looking for a man called Nestor,' said Lena. 'Where does he live?'

'Nestor?' repeated the boy. 'Not heard of him.'

Berry's hand went to her knife and the boy's eyes widened again.

'Honestly! I swear! I've lived here all my life! I'm not lying! I'm not! You're mad!'

'He's not lying!' chimed the other two boys.

'I think they're telling the truth,' said Berry. She leaned into the boy, her nose almost touching his. 'Yep, definitely telling the truth. You wouldn't lie to me, would you?'

The boy shook his head enthusiastically.

The other two boys slowly got to their feet as Lena watched them, just in case.

'What about him in the woods?' said one of the boys.

'Oh! Yeah!' said the bigger boy. 'There's a bloke there who lives on his own. Don't know his name though. He never comes to town. It could be him! I'm sure it is!'

'Okay,' Lena replied. 'Take us to him.'

'No way!' cried the boy.

Berry sighed and took out her knife.

'We can't!' said one of the other boys. 'We don't know where he lives exactly! It's a bit difficult to find him as anyone who goes near his place comes back to town a bit…different.'

'Different?' said Silas. 'How?'

'Look,' said the bigger boy. 'Are you in any rush?'

Lena's eyes narrowed. 'Yes. Why?'

'Well, you look a state and we can help. And we can tell you about this Nestor too. We've got a house, hot food, beds…'

Lena suddenly felt every ache from their journey to Ivanmoon. 'I suppose we could spare an hour or two…'

'It's not a trap,' said the bigger boy. 'You're more than welcome to stay out here if you like though - your choice.'

Lena looked at the sky. The clouds were looking even darker and heavier than before. It would be throwing it down before long.

'Okay,' said Lena. 'But if you do anything…'

Berry drew her finger across her throat and made a horrible sound.

'Nothing will happen!' said the boy.

'There are others too,' said Lena.

'Go get them!' said the boy. 'Rancy will go with you and show you where we live.'

The bigger boy nodded to one of the smaller boys. The knights left the bigger boy and his friend and went back to the others. Rancy came with them. He looked too scared to say anything as they made their way through the pine forest to where the other squires were waiting.

'Where are your parents?' asked Silas, wanting to break the silence as they walked.

'Gone,' said Rancy.

'Where?' asked Berry.

'The wars,' said Rancy. 'Almost everyone got sent and no one has come back.'

'They're dead?'

Rancy shrugged. 'Don't know. Maybe. They're gone; that's all we know. They tried to take all the orphans too but we hid and the soldiers didn't find us. We don't want to end up dead on a battlefield too.'

They got back to the other squires and told them what had happened. The others looked wary but it was obvious they could do with somewhere warm to sleep.

'Come on,' said Rancy. He looked up at the sky and raindrops appeared on his cheeks and forehead. 'It'll get dark soon. It's best not to be out here at night.'

# Chapter Eighteen

Rancy led the group back to Ivanmoon and then to a small abandoned-looking house at the edge of town. Inside, they found the older boy they had met at the fountain as well as more boys and girls. They were all gathered together.

'It's not much,' said the older boy, welcoming them in. 'But it's ours.

Lena looked around the main room. It was tatty and a little dusty but it looked homely enough. Beds were placed around the walls and in the centre was a table with chairs packed around it. Against one wall was a fireplace with a roaring fire. Lena wanted to get closer to it as soon as possible.

'Doesn't anyone mind you living here?' she asked.

'Nah,' said the older boy. 'There are quite a few empty houses here. The Ivanmoon Scruffers aren't a burden on anyone and we earn our food.'

'Ivanmoon Scruffers?' said Silas.

'That's what we call ourselves,' the boy replied. 'My name's Hounslow by the way.' The boy stuck out his hand awkwardly and Lena shook it.

'I'm Lena,' said Lena. She went on to introduce the rest of the squires. 'And the girl who had her knife to your throat is Berry. Look, sorry about what happened in the square. It's been a hard couple of weeks.'

'Nice to meet you,' said Hounslow. 'And don't worry about it. And nice to meet you too, Berry.' He looked at Berry a little longer than any of the others.

Berry frowned at him and gave him a quick nod.

'Alright?' she sniffed.

'You should eat,' Hounslow continued. 'Sit, sit!'

A couple of the other children ran to another room and brought out steaming pots. They placed them in the middle of the table and another boy put bowls and spoons around the edges. Only Hounslow then sat at the table; the rest sat on the beds along the room's walls.

'Sorry but we don't have room for all of you at the table. Some of you will have to sit with the others,' said Hounslow.

Lena and the others sat wherever they could as quickly as possible. She took a place at the table and Silas and Berry sat either side of her. They let the rich smells that drifted from the pots waft into their noses. Lena's mouth watered and her stomach grumbled.

Hounslow dished out the hot, thick soup and Lena stared at it. The soup glooped and swirled and bits of meat and vegetables bobbed to the surface; it looked wonderful. After living on berries and whatever animals they could catch on their way here, it was all she could do not to pick up the bowl and swallow the soup down in one go. She picked up her spoon and began to eat. After the first sip, Lena thanked Hounslow then asked: 'This man in the woods…'

'He's lived there for as long as I can remember,' Hounslow replied. He rocked back in his chair and patted his stomach. 'I've never seen him though. He's never come to town and no one goes to see him except Julienna.'

'Who's Julienna?' asked Silas. He was getting the soup inside of himself almost as fast as Lena.

'She works at the grocery shop in town,' Hounslow replied. 'She takes him food every week. You're in luck; she's taking him his things tomorrow.'

'You said anyone else who goes to see him comes back different,' said Lena.

'Not different exactly,' Hounslow replied. He turned to the other children in the room. 'Gabrielle, come here.'

A young girl of about eight got up and stood next to Hounslow. She wore a faded dress and in her hands was a doll with one eye missing.

'Gabrielle, tell them what happened when you went to find that bloke in the wood's house.'

Gabrielle looked down at the floor and began to speak: 'I was walking in the woods for a bit, having a look around. There was a rustle in some bushes and I went over to see what it was. Then I woke up on the edge of the woods near town.'

'What happened?' asked Lena.

'Don't know,' Gabrielle replied.

'She wasn't hurt,' said Hounslow. 'But she can't remember anything, can you Gabrielle?'

Gabrielle shook her head.

'And sometimes she goes a bit distant on us. It's a bit weird but there you go. Is this Nestor definitely in Ivanmoon?' asked Hounslow.

'I'm sure of it,' said Lena.

'Then it must be him. There's no one else here called that. Tomorrow, Julienna will go into the woods to deliver his food. We'll follow her and see what happens.'

'Okay,' said Lena, she was wary of this Hounslow, but she was too tired to argue. She could feel her eyelids droop and her body felt heavy. It was getting very dark outside and the rain was now battering the windows. Lena was glad they were not out there, at least.

'There are rooms upstairs with enough bedding for your lot,' said Hounslow. 'Come on, I'll show you.'

Hounslow led the squires upstairs. It was colder than the room with the fire but it was far better than where they had slept every night since leaving the Twisted Keep. On the floor were mats and blankets, enough for all the squires to wrap up snug and warm.

'Thank you,' said Lena.

'It's okay,' said Hounslow.

'You haven't asked who we are,' said Berry.

'No,' replied Hounslow. 'That's your business.'

Hounslow left the room and the squires bedded down.

'Do you trust him?' asked Berry.

'I think so,' Lena replied. 'But just in case,' she looked at the squires. 'Lizzy, you take first watch. Gregory you take over after and Michael you're last.'

The squires got themselves ready and pulled the blankets over themselves. Before Lena closed her eyes she looked at Lizzy. The young girl was staring at the door with eyes of steel. They would be safe tonight.

They slept.

****

Hours later, Lena woke to screaming. Eyes wide but still half-asleep, she looked round. The other squires were waking up too and they all look startled.

'Report!' she hissed in the darkness, but whoever was meant to be on watch wasn't there.

Lena grabbed her sword, got up and crossed the room. The screaming was coming from downstairs. Lena opened the door to their room a fraction and looked outside. The corridor was dark and she couldn't hear any noise other than the crying.

'What's going on?' asked Silas, wiping the sleep from his eyes.

'I don't know,' said Lena. 'It could be Erin though. Get ready for a fight.' She looked around and saw Michael Obasi wasn't there. Third watch. Maybe four in the morning then.

The squires gathered their weapons and the screaming continued. Lena opened the bedroom door and crept downstairs. The other squires followed her.

At the bottom of the stairs, Lena pushed a door open and peered into the room where they had eaten only hours before. Suddenly the door opened further and Rancy was standing there. He cried out at the sight of the Order's swords.

'It's just us!' said Lena.

'Sorry,' said Rancy. 'It's Gabrielle.'

Lena sighed with relief and told the other squires to relax. Rancy turned and went back into the main room. Lena and the others followed him.

On one of the beds sat Gabrielle. Hounslow had his arms around her and she sobbed into his shoulder. Michael Obasi stood near the door.

'I wanted to check it out before I woke you,' said Michael.

Lena nodded to the squire. 'What's going on?

There was a bang and the front door opened. One of the other Ivanmoon Scruffers came in.

'Are you okay, Gabby?' asked the girl who entered. 'I don't know how it got in.'

'What's going on?' asked Lena, annoyed she had been ignored the first time.

Hounslow looked up. 'A cat got into the house,' he explained.

'What's wrong with that?' asked Silas.

'When Gabrielle came back from the woods after what happened, she also started being really scared of cats,' explained Hounslow. 'We've got no idea why but as soon as she sees one she starts screaming. A tabby managed to get in here and curled up on her bed. It terrified her. You're okay now though, aren't you Gabby?'

Gabby lifted her head and nodded.

'That *is* strange,' said Silas.

'Let's go back to sleep,' said Lena. 'Tomorrow sounds like it's going to be an interesting day.' Lena went up to Gabrielle.

'And you see him there?' Lena pointed at Michael. 'He'll stay here for the rest of the night to make sure no more cats get in, okay?'

Gabrielle looked at Michael then at his sword. 'Okay,' she said.

Michael went to the centre of the room, faced the door that led outside, then sat crossed-legged and laid his sword across his legs. Lena and the others left and Gabrielle climbed back into bed.

# Chapter Nineteen

The next morning the squires were up and ready when Hounslow knocked on their door and entered.

'You're up,' said Hounslow. 'Good. Julienna will be leaving soon.'

Lena looked at the squires. 'Berry, Silas, come with me. Everyone else, stay here. We'll be back soon.'

Hounslow led the three squires out of the house and into the streets. They made their way back to the main square and sat at the fountain. Hounslow pointed to a shop on the edge of the square that had a sign hanging outside.

'That's Julienna's shop,' said Hounslow. 'She'll be leaving soon. Watch.'

They waited for ten minutes or so and sure enough the door to the shop opened. Out came a woman holding a basket.

'That's her,' said Hounslow.

Julienna made her way out of the square.

'Let's go,' said Lena.

The squires began to move and Hounslow came with them.

'Where do you think you're going?' asked Berry.

'I'm coming with you,' replied Hounslow. 'I want to see what happens.'

'No, you're not,' said Berry.

'Let him, Berry,' said Lena. 'He knows this place better than we do and we owe him one.'

Berry stared daggers at Hounslow and turned away. 'Fine,' she huffed.

The squires and Hounslow followed Julienna out of town, over a bridge that crossed a fast-running stream, and into the dense woods that surrounded the village. The path Julienna took snaked between the pine trees. Lena saw Julienna's feet disappear into the morning mist as she got further away.

The squires kept as far back as they could. They stayed off the path and used the trees and bushes to keep out of sight as much as possible. Every footfall done gently to make sure they didn't tread on any twigs or kick any stones that would alert Julienna, or anyone else, that they were there.

After maybe thirty minutes, Julienna turned sharply and disappeared behind a broad pine tree. The squires moved quickly but when they reached the tree Julienna had vanished.

'She's gone!' hissed Silas.

'Do you see any tracks?' asked Lena.

Silas moved away from the other squires to where they last saw Julienna, He looked at the ground.

'Here,' he said. 'This-'

But before Silas could finish there was a screech, a cry, and a flash of silver. Something big had attacked and Silas was on the floor. Whatever had hit him had disappeared into the bushes again.

'What happened?!' Silas shouted.

He lay on the ground, dazed. Lena, Berry and Hounslow ran towards him.

'No idea,' said Lena. 'Are you all right?'

Silas got up and the squires drew their swords; Hounslow pulled an evil-looking cleaver from his belt.

There was another screech and out of nowhere a great beast appeared. It crashed into the squires, knocking them down. It turned and stopped. Lena could now see it clearly.

'What is *that!!!?*' cried Hounslow.

The thing in front of them was close to the size of an archon, covered in metal and it didn't look friendly. It also looked oddly familiar.

'Is that a *cat*?' said Berry.

Lena agreed. The creature did indeed look like a cat, albeit the biggest any of them had ever seen. But it wasn't made of flesh and bone.

'It's not alive,' said Lena. 'It's a machine!'

The mechanical cat snarled at the squires and rushed towards them; bounding forward with paws and claws outstretched. It went for Lena. She rolled to the right, avoiding the paw that would have crashed down on her stomach had she been slower.

The others had got back up.

'Help!' cried Lena.

Berry looked at Lena then got closer to the cat, looking for a spot that might weaken it or slow it down, but she couldn't see one.

'How?' Berry shouted back.

The cat turned and took a swipe at Berry. Lena heard a screech as its claws raked across her armour. Berry jumped back.

On the floor, Lena felt something wet on her side. Was she bleeding? She reached down, fearing the worst, but when her hand came back she saw that it was covered in oil rather than blood. Her travel lantern had broken. Lena sighed with relief.

Meanwhile, Hounslow was moving around the cat.

'What do we do?!' he cried and the cat turned to him.

'Distract it!' shouted Berry.

Hounslow saw stones and twigs on the floor. He grabbed a handful and started throwing them at the cat. Each one hit the creature with a *clank*. The cat padded forward towards Hounslow.

'Do whatever you're going to do now!' he called to Berry

Lena could only watch as Berry rounded the beast while its attention was on Hounslow.

*She isn't...* thought Lena.

Berry ran and jumped on the creature's back. The mechanical cat went wild; bucking and trying to shake the squire off.

*She's mad,* Lena said to herself. She got back up and rushed over to Silas.

'Are you okay?' she asked, pulling him up.

'Yeah,' said Silas, 'just winded that's all.'

They turned back to the cat. Berry was still perched on top of it; one hand holding an ear and the other holding her sword.

'There's nowhere to stab it!' cried Berry. 'It's just armour plates up here!'

The cat was going berserk and all Lena, Silas and Hounslow could do was watch as Berry tried to hold on. Suddenly, it smashed itself against a tree and Berry flew off.

'Ooofff!' cried Berry as she hit a tree and crumpled to the ground. The cat then pounced on her, its paws now on her arms.

'Berry!!' cried Lena.

'Alice! Stop!' said a voice. The mechanical cat moved its paws off Berry and sat down next to her as if nothing had happened.

Lena, Silas and Hounslow turned to see who had spoken. Berry picked herself up.

Standing behind them was an old man. He had scraggly grey hair, dirty clothes and a straw hat on his head. He was also very thin and had a weather-beaten face. He wasn't much taller than the squires either.

'Nestor?' said Lena.

'Aye,' said Nestor. 'And I'm guessing Sir Poland sent you.'

# Chapter Twenty

Nestor led the squires to a small cottage that sat in the middle of a clearing. Ivy climbed the cottage walls. A tumbledown well and vegetable garden was nearby. Lena imagined a witch living there rather than this odd old man.

'So this is where you live?' asked Lena.

'Yep,' said Nestor. 'It's not a bad little place.'

'Where's Julienna?' asked Hounslow.

'Been and gone,' Nestor replied. 'Who do you think told me you lot were playing with Alice?'

Alice, the mechanical cat, trotted along next to them. When they got to the cottage she leapt onto its roof, curled up, and looked as if she had fallen sleep.

'Don't mind her,' said Nestor. 'She'll come down when she's ready. Come in and wipe your feet.'

The squires entered the cottage and wiped their feet. Inside, the cottage was more workshop than home. Nuts and bolts lay everywhere; cogs were stacked in high piles and books littered the floor and filled the shelves. In one corner was a small bed and in another was a stove with a frying pan on top of it. Lena looked up at the roof and could see dust drift down as Alice shifted position. The whole cottage creaked.

'Sit,' said Nestor, pointing at the bed.

The squires and Hounslow sat down and Nestor took a stool, pushed the papers and gears off it, and joined them.

'Sorry about Alice,' said Nestor. 'She gets a bit carried away. She wouldn't have hurt you though. What's happened?'

Lena told Nestor what had happened at the Twisted Keep.

Nestor listened; his face a grim mask.

'Then it's begun,' said Nestor sadly.

'Who are you?' asked Berry. 'I've never seen you at the Twisted Keep.'

Nestor reached into his tattered shirt and pulled out something. It was a medallion just like the one Sir Poland had given Lena.

'You're a knight?' said Silas.

'Used to be,' said Nestor. 'Too old now.'

'What are you doing here?' asked Lena.

'I'm retired,' Nestor replied. 'I came here for some peace and quiet. It looks like that's about to change though.'

'Sir Poland wanted us to find you,' said Lena. 'Why?'

'Ah, well, you see you never really leave the Order; even at my age. Do you know what a fail-safe is?'

The squires nodded.

'It's a back-up plan,' said Lena. 'In case something goes wrong.'

'That's right,' said Nestor. 'Just in case anything happened to the Twisted Keep and the Order.'

'What do we do now?' asked Silas. 'Sir Poland didn't tell us anything.'

'That was for the best. Alberghast does like to keep his cards close to his chest,' said Nestor. 'Probably sensible on this occasion though.'

'Do you know him well?' asked Lena.

Nestor rocked back and laughed. 'Oh, I know Sir Alberghast Poland, my dear! Who do you think taught him everything he knows?'

'Eh?' said Lena.

'Sir Poland was this man's squire,' explained Berry.

'Aye, that he was,' said Nestor. 'A pain in my backside as well most of the time!'

The squires laughed. They couldn't imagine Sir Poland as

a squire.

'He was always running into a fight without thinking that one,' Nestor continued. 'Always had to be the best and bravest. There was more than one time I had to get him out of a hairy situation! Daft boy.'

'He's still the same,' said Lena.

'I bet he is,' Nestor laughed.

'You're- you're from the *Order of the Furnace?*' said Hounslow. He stared at Nestor and the squires.

'Yep,' said Lena.

Hounslow's mouth dropped open. 'You're famous!' he stuttered.

Lena shrugged her shoulders and turned back to Nestor. 'We came straight from the Keep,' said Lena. 'I have Sir Poland's Archon too.'

'Pandora's here?' cried Nestor.' Wonderful! I must see her at once!'

'What are we going to do about Erin and the King ?' asked Berry. She sounded impatient.

'Ah, well, I'm just one part of the fail-safe. Now we need to go somewhere first. There's an abandoned castle called Fallengarden, close to the city of Jultsthorne,' said Nestor.

'What's there?' asked Lena.

'It's best I don't tell you, just in case you find yourself in the dungeons of Casenberg. I bet Erin is scouring the land looking for you' said Nestor. 'But, if that happens and you manage to get away, make your way to Fallengarden as fast as you can. It's the only place in the empire you might be safe right now and all will be explained.'

The door creaked open and Alice strode in. Once inside, she gently kicked the front door closed behind her and then curled up in one corner.

'What *is* that?' asked Hounslow.

She's here to protect me,' Nestor replied.

'It's a soul-machine,' said Lena.

'*She* if you don't mind, and yes *she* is. A bit of a pet project of mine after I left the Order. She's good at keeping people away so I can work.'

'I think I know why Gabrielle is so scared of cats now,' muttered Hounslow.

Nestor stood up. 'Right, we should make a move. Are there more of you?'

'Yes,' said Lena. 'They're in Ivanmoon.'

'We'll go and get them first then,' said Nestor. 'We need to be quick.'

Nestor got up and went outside. The squires and Hounslow followed.

At the rear of the cottage was a cart. A shire horse stood tethered to a tree nearby. Nestor untied the horse and attached it to the cart. He went back inside and came out again with two sacks.

'It'll be a long journey' he said. He went back and forth a few times more, bringing more sacks each time. Finally, he brought a small wooden chest and placed in carefully in the wagon. Once he had finished he looked at Alice who now was trotting about outside.

'Get in,' he said, pointing at the cart. Alice leapt onto the cart and curled up. Nestor then grabbed a tarpaulin and threw it over the mechanical cat and the other items, hiding her and them from sight.

'What about us?' asked Hounslow.

Nestor climbed onto the driver's seat, geed the shire-horse and the cart started moving.

'You'll be walking,' he said.

# Chapter Twenty-One

Nestor, Hounslow and the squires made their way through the woods to Ivanmoon. Hounslow then led them to the orphans' house where the other squires were waiting. When Nestor's cart stopped outside, both Hounslow's gang and the squires came out of the house.

'Is that him? Is that Nestor?' asked Ton Singh. He and the other squires peered at Nestor curiously.

'Yes,' Lena replied. 'All of you, get your things. We're moving.'

The squires went back inside the house.

'Hey!'

Lena turned to see Rancy running towards her. He looked worried.

'What's wrong?' asked Hounslow when Rancy got to them.

Rancy stopped, bent double and tried to catch his breath.

'Soldiers!' he gasped. 'Here!'

'What are they doing?' asked Berry.

'They've been going door-to-door,' Rancy answered. 'They're looking for you. They'll be here in five minutes maybe!'

'Where are your horses?' asked Nestor.

'They're off the road going out of the valley,' said Lena. 'It's not far.'

'Then let's go!' said Nestor.

Lena looked at Hounslow. 'What's the fastest way out of town?'

'I'll show you,' said Hounslow. He turned to Rancy.

'Rancy, I need you and the others to slow the soldiers down.'

Rancy nodded and smiled. 'No worries, boss!'

Lena watched Rancy and the rest of the Ivanmoon Scruffers run off down an alley next to their home. 'Will they be okay?' she asked Hounslow.

'Yeah, I expect so,' Hounslow replied. 'They know what they're doing. Come on, let's go!'

Nestor got his cart moving again and the squires started running. Lena looked back and wished the Ivanmoon Scruffers the best of luck.

Nestor and the squires made their way out of Ivanmoon as quickly as they could; their eyes darted about all the time, looking out for any royal soldiers that would give them away. Luckily, no one saw them and they went into the forest without difficulty.

They found the horses and Pandora where they had left them, and the few squires left on guard.
Nestor, upon seeing Pandora, slid off his cart and ran over to the Archon. He put a hand on her mane and Pandora lowered her head.

'It's been a long time, old girl,' said Nestor softly.

'You know her?' asked Lena.

'She used to be mine,' said Nestor. 'She passed to Sir Poland when I left the Twisted Keep.'

'Do...do you want to ride her?' asked Lena.

Nestor looked at Lena closely. 'No, squire. Sir Poland passed her to you. I wouldn't dream of taking another knight's archon.'

'Thanks,' said Lena. And you'll have to tell me all about your time with her.'

'We've got a long ride,' said Nestor. 'We'll have time.'

Hounslow appeared next to Lena. He looked back towards town. 'That was close!' he said. He then looked at

Lena seriously. 'Look, I know I'm not one of you but...'

'You're coming with us,' said Lena. 'No arguments.'

'Great!' said Hounslow. He looked ahead with a smile on his face.

'You have to,' said Lena. 'You know where we're going and I can't let the Royal Army get hold of you, so it's coming with us or...'

Hounslow looked at Lena wide-eyed when he realized what she meant.

'You wouldn't.'

Lena laughed. 'No, of course not. I'd feel bad.'

'Phew!'

'I'd get Berry to do it.'

Hounslow looked at Berry and Berry winked at him.

The squires got on their mounts, leaving Hounslow standing alone. 'What should I do?' he asked Lena.

'You can ride with me if you want,' said Berry. She tapped the space on her horse behind her.

'Er...'

'Join me,' said Nestor. He moved away from Pandora and on to the wagon again. 'Get on.'

Hounslow climbed onto the seat at the front of the cart next to Nestor. He then looked back at the tarpaulin that covered Alice. Alice shifted under the tarpaulin and Lena saw Hounslow jump a little. 'I suppose this is better,' he said quietly.

# Chapter Twenty-Two

It had been three weeks since Sir Poland and the other knights of the Order had been taken to Casenberg. Once they had arrived they had been led down into the depths of the glorious, bannered city to its cruel dungeons, from where no one is said ever to have escaped.

Sir Poland was led to a small dark cell that contained a stinking brown blanket and a bucket. He stepped inside and the metal door slammed shut behind him.

For the next few weeks he saw and heard no one except for a guard who would push food into his cell once a day and replace the bucket. Then, one day, four guards came, chained his hands behind his back and led him out of his cell.

Sir Poland grunted as he was pushed through a door into a small, bleak room with no windows. The room's walls were made of grey, unhappy stone and in the middle of the room was a wooden table and two chairs.

On one of the chairs sat Erin. She looked at Sir Poland calmly; her back straight and her delicate hands resting on the table. Her face was a mask.

'Sir Poland,' said Erin, her smooth skin barely creasing. 'I hope you are well.'

Sir Poland ignored Erin and sat down.

'I asked are you well?' said Erin.

Sir Poland continued to ignore her.

Erin sighed. 'We will find your squires, Sir Poland, they cannot possibly hide from us. It's just a matter of time.'

Erin placed a note on the table in front of Sir Poland. Sir Poland looked down.

*'The squires have been seen in Ivanmoon,'* read the note. *'Enquiries are proceeding.'*

'See?' said Erin. 'So they went to Ivanmoon, did they? That's rather odd, isn't it? What could be in that little backwater that would be of importance to the Order I wonder? Why don't you tell me? If you *do* tell me, I might be able to keep them alive. We have their families too, did you know that? They can have normal lives if they give up. They won't be soldiers of course, but they won't be in the ground either.'

She waited.

And waited some more.

'No? Then you condemn them to die.' Erin stood up and went to the door.

'You won't beat us,' said Sir Poland.

'What was that?' asked Erin.

'You won't beat us, Vulture.'

Erin laughed. 'We already have, Sir Poland.'

'You're scared, Erin,' said Sir Poland grimly. 'I can smell it on you. You're scared of a few *children*.'

Erin smiled. 'Goodbye, my lord,' she said and left the room.

When Erin stepped out of the room and into the corridor, the smile on her face vanished. She turned to the guards who were now standing to attention.

'Take him back to his cell,' Erin commanded.

She made her way down the corridor to the golden elevator at the far end of the dungeons. She pressed the 'call' button, waited a few moments, then the doors opened and she stepped inside.

'The Royal apartments,' she said to the porter.

The porter sat on a stool with the elevator controls in his hand. He nodded, pulled a lever, and the elevator doors closed. After a minute or so the doors opened again and Erin stepped out, turned, and strode forward. She came to a set of ornate double doors beside which stood two guards. The guards took one look at her and opened the doors without saying a word. Erin stepped through.

When she was through the doors, Erin gagged as they closed behind her. The smell was appalling today; the royal apartment was as disgusting as usual. Dust lay everywhere and little sunlight made it through the grimy windows. The smell of rot filled her nostrils, making her stomach turn and her skin crawl. She pulled out a cloth and put it to her mouth and nose.

'Your majesty?' she called into the gloom.

'Here, Erin,' came a voice from the next room. Erin made her way towards it while trying not to breathe.

In the next room was a great four-poster bed. Drapes covered the sides so it was impossible to see past them. On the drapes were lots of black spots: dead flies, Erin noticed. The smell was even worse in here.

'My King,' said Erin. 'I have spoken to Sir Poland.'

'And?' said the voice from behind the drapes.

'He won't say anything,' Erin replied.

'And why has he and the others not been put to death?' questioned the King .

'For a number of reasons, my King. First: we cannot get any of their machines to work. Second: my soldiers reported Sir Poland specifically helped the squires to escape and I want to know why. And third: to execute the knights so soon after we attacked them will make you look like a tyrant.'

'A tyrant? Me?'

There was a gargling sound that Erin took to be a laugh.

'The empire is fragile, my King, and we don't need any more reasons for rebellion. We must be seen to treat them fairly.'

Fingers appeared at the drapes; gnarled talons of hands. They pulled the drapes back and the King stepped into the room. Erin stepped back in horror and quickly lowered her eyes.

'My King, you are not well, you must rest.'

King Claudio stepped closer, bringing with him the smell of rotting meat and the buzzing of flies.

'Erin,' said the King . He reached out and placed a stinking hand on Erin's cheek. 'Do what is best, but there can be no loose ends for the coming war. Make me proud.'

Of- of course, my King,' Erin stammered.

She felt her skin under the King's hand start to burn and itch. She wanted to tear the King's hand away and run out of the room.

'You may leave,' said the King .

King Claudio turned and returned to his bed. The dirty dressing gown hanging from his shoulders slid along behind him, leaving a glistening trail on the floor. Erin felt her throat tighten.

Erin bowed and then turned and left. She moved quickly through the apartment until she got to the guarded door. She went through it and found one of the guards holding a paper bag.

She took the bag from the guard and threw up into it. When she had finished she looked up to see Yvette, her assistant, waiting for her.

'You've heard?' asked Erin, passing the now full bag back to the guard.

Yvette nodded.

'Send out the Jasareen,' ordered Erin. 'They are to leave no stone unturned. Find those children.'

# Chapter Twenty-Three

'We make camp here!' Lena called out. She stopped Pandora and dismounted, as did the other squires.

They had halted at the base of a group of hills that were covered in a few trees, bushes and coarse yellowing grass. There was a stream nearby so they and the horses could drink, and the hills meant the wind would be kept off them whilst they rested. It was a good place to stop.

'We're not far now,' said Nestor, jumping off his cart. 'These are the Yellowback hills and Jultsthorne is just over the rise there. After that, it's just a few days' ride to Fallengarden.'

'Good,' said Lena. 'Maybe then we can find out what we're going to do.'

The journey to the Yellowback hills had been fairly straightforward. They had left the valley of Ivanmoon and had travelled cross-country for three weeks. Also, during that time, Alice the mechanical cat was introduced to the rest of the squires. She remained in Nestor's cart for the entire journey as the squires couldn't risk anyone else seeing her; she was too strange and word could get back to Erin.

During the journey, Lena had been impressed by Hounslow. He helped whenever he could and learned how to set up camp, hunt and do all the things the other squires would do while travelling very quickly. He had even started practicing with a sword.

Now the squires prepared their camp once again. They unrolled their bedding, lit cooking fires, and then gathered around the fires to keep warm and to talk to one another. A few went hunting and half an hour later came back with rabbits to eat. Lena gave orders to those who would be on watch overnight.

Lena sat next to Silas. He was hunched up and looking into the fire. Lena noticed he had been getting a lot quieter over the past few days.

'What's wrong?' asked Lena.

'I grew up in Jultsthorne,' Silas replied. 'It's been ages since I've been this close to it.'

Lena didn't know what to say next. She had been lucky. She had been brought up by her parents and the knights had recruited her while she was at school. They had even moved her parents to Upsalom so they could be close to Lena. Silas had had a very different life. He had been living on the streets of Jultsthorne for years before joining the Order. Lena couldn't even imagine what that must have been like.

'There's no reason to go there,' said Lena softly. 'We'll go around it in the morning. With any luck you won't even see the walls.'

Silas nodded. 'I still know it's there though.' He turned, looked at Lena and climbed into his travel blanket. 'Night, Lena.'

'Night, Silas,' said Lena. She watched him close his eyes and then she climbed into her own bedding.

The fires slowly died down, the stars came out, and the squires slept.

That night, Berry was on watch. She walked to the edge of the camp, up one of the hills and looked out over the countryside. Night was setting in properly now but her thick clothes were keeping most of the cold out. Across the hills she could see the occasional flickering of farmhouse candles and hear the gentle sound of the mooing of cows floating on the wind. To her left was a glow coming over the hills: Jultsthorne.

She heard movement behind her. She spun round, her

sword drawn.

'Who's there?' she called out.

'It's just me,' said Hounslow, appearing from the darkness.

'What are you doing here?' asked Berry. 'You're not on duty.'

'I can't sleep,' replied Hounslow. 'I thought you might be thirsty too.' In his hand were two mugs. He passed one to Berry. She took it and sipped: tea.

'Thanks,' said Berry.

She started walking slowly and Hounslow joined her.

'So what's it like?' Hounslow asked.

'What's what like?' Berry replied.

'Being in the Order of the Furnace? I can't believe I'm riding with you- the Order I mean. You're famous! We tell stories about you in Ivanmoon.'

'You're asking now?' said Berry. 'We've been riding together for weeks.'

'I didn't have the courage,' said Hounslow. 'I've spoken to the others but not you; you're a bit scary if I'm honest.'

Berry snorted. 'Am I? Sorry.' She then thought for a moment. 'It's the best thing in the world,' she replied. 'It was, anyway.'

'Tell me about it.'

'I don't know…'

'Please? When I get back to Ivanmoon everyone will want to hear.'

Berry sighed. 'Okay, did anyone say anything about the Desert Kingdom of the Kragger-lyn?'

'No. Where's that?'

Berry looked up at the stars then pointed to her right. 'About five hundred miles that way,' she said. 'Or at least it used to be.'

'Used to be?'

'It's part of the empire now,' said Berry. 'We won, but only just. Do you know what Drazarks are?'

'Nope.'

'Sandworms,' said Berry. 'The Kragger-lyn ride them into battle. A hundred soldiers can ride on the back of one and they can eat a mounted knight whole.'

'They must be terrifying!' said Hounslow.

Berry shrugged. 'I suppose. They aren't very bright though.'

Hounslow and Berry stood for a while and Berry told Hounslow more about the battles she had seen and the places she had visited. Hounslow hung on her every word.

After a while, Hounslow started to yawn despite himself. 'You'll have to carry on tomorrow. I think I need to sleep.'

'All right,' said Berry. 'Night.'

'Thanks. Night.' Hounslow turned to go.

Berry watched Hounslow vanish down the side of the hill she was standing on. She then started her patrol around the camp. She went up and down the other hills around the squires' camp, looking for anything suspicious.

At the top of one, she paused. There was rushing sound behind her.

*What's Hounslow up to now?* She thought to herself.

But as Berry moved huge hands clamped onto her. One covered her mouth and the other held her arms by her side. She was lifted her into the air. She kicked at the legs of whoever had grabbed her and beat at the arm over her mouth, but it was no use; it was like fighting an oak tree.

'Got her, boss,' said a gruff voice near Berry's head. Whoever it was, his breath smelled awful.

Berry was swung around by the man and now, in front of her, she saw an old woman. The woman was bent over a walking stick and her head was wrapped in a woollen shawl. Poking out of the shawl was a wrinkled face and long nose.

'Well done, Douglas,' said the woman. 'And it looks like

she's got a lot of fight in her.

'Yeah, she's struggling like a real live one!' said the man called Douglas.

'She'll make a pretty penny for us. And there's me thinking tonight was going to be a waste.'

The woman began to walk away and the man called Douglas followed, carrying Berry.

# Chapter Twenty-Four

'Lena! Wake up!'

Lena's eyes flew open. Silas was standing over her. He looked frantic.

'What is it? What's happened?' Lena scrambled out of her bedding and onto her feet. Around her everyone else was still sleeping and the fire were barely glowing.

'It's Berry!' said Silas. 'She's gone!'

'She can't be,' said Lena.

'We've not heard from her in hours.'

'What about Aisha?' asked Lena. 'Wasn't she on watch too?'

'She says she needed the loo. She's really sorry.'

Lena groaned. 'Show me where she was last seen.'

Lena grabbed a sword, tied it to her back and threw a cloak over herself to keep out the morning cold. They then began walking through the camp. While doing so, Nestor approached them. He was wearing woolly pyjamas and a cap on his head.

'What's wrong?' he asked.

Lena told him what had happened. 'I'm coming with you,' said Nestor.

Silas took them up one of the hills. At the top of the hill they found Hounslow moving around, looking at the ground.

'They got her here,' said Hounslow, his voice shaking.

'They?' asked Lena.

'Two people,' said Hounslow. 'Someone really big and someone else much smaller. They went this way.'

Hounslow led Lena, Silas and Nestor down the other side

of the hill to where a dirt road ran through the hills. He bent down at the side of the road.

'Wagon tracks,' said Hounslow.

Nestor put his hand to his forehead and looked at the horizon. 'I think I know who it was,' he said.

'Who?' asked Lena.

'Slavers.'

Silas went pale. 'This is really bad, Lena, really, *really* bad.'

'We'll get her back,' said Lena, patting Silas on the shoulder. She looked at Nestor. 'Where have they have taken her?'

'Back to Jultsthorne I imagine,' said Nestor.

'Looks like that's where we're going then,' said Lena. She felt angry but tried not to show it. A delay was the last thing they needed.

'We'll never get through the gates,' said Nestor. 'The guards might be on the look-out for us.'

'We can't leave her there!' cried Hounslow.

'No one is saying that,' said Lena. 'Ideas anyone?'

'I can get us in,' said Silas. 'Just us two though.'

'Okay.' Lena looked at Hounslow and Nestor. 'Look after the camp until we return. Keep an eye on each other and make sure no one else gets taken. If we're not back by tonight make your way to Fallengarden and we'll meet you there.'

Nestor and Hounslow nodded and left without argument. Hounslow looked calmer now.

'What do we do now?' Lena asked Silas.

'Follow me,' said Silas.

# Chapter Twenty-Five

Fifteen minutes later, Lena and Silas saw Jultsthorne. The sun was completely over the horizon now and the sky was cloudy. Jultsthorne was a massive, sprawling city surrounded by high stone walls that still bore the scars of old wars. From a distance the city didn't look that big, but as they got closer Lena realised just how huge it was.

'It's going to be hard finding Berry in that,' Lena said glumly as they made their way along the dirt road that led around the city.

'I think I know where she might have been taken,' Silas replied. He veered off the road and headed towards the eastern side of the city. Lena followed him.

When they arrived at the walls of Jultsthorne, Silas got very close to the wall and knelt in the grass. He reached down, pulled, and Lena saw a metal grate appeared in his hands.

Lena looked over Silas' shoulder and saw he had uncovered a hole in the ground.

'What is it?' asked Lena

'A rat-street,' said Silas. 'They run all over the city and out into the countryside. They're perfect for people wanting to get around or in and out of Jultsthorne without being seen.'

Silas jumped straight down the hole. Lena did the same and below, she found herself in a long, dark tunnel.

'Silas? Are you there?' Lena called out.

There was a spark and a flash. Silas' face appeared above a flickering flame. They were at the beginning of a long tunnel.

'Lead the way,' said Lena.

They made their way down the rat-street. It was damp and smelled awful and Lena couldn't see a single source of light other than Silas' lantern.

'How do you know about these tunnels?' asked Lena.

'I used them a lot when I lived here,' Silas replied. 'Keep your eyes peeled.'

Lena was about to ask why but then she heard a squeak next to her. She turned and could just about make out the shape of the biggest rat she had ever seen crawling only centimeters from her face. It looked at her, hissed and scurried off, its claws rat-at-tatting down the tunnel.

'I hate rats,' muttered Lena.

'Better than snakes,' Silas replied.

Silas brought the lantern down towards the floor and Lena shuddered. Lena could see long, scaled tails disappear into cracks and holes in the tunnel wall. She was glad she had her thick boots on.

'Just watch your-' began Silas, but he didn't get a chance to finish. There was a crack, a cry, and he vanished into the floor with a *whoosh*.

'Silas!' cried Lena.

She jumped forward but she was too late. She looked down and saw Silas and the lantern he was holding disappear down the hole in the floor. Lena was now in complete darkness.

'Silas? Can you hear me?' Lena called out, trying to stay calm. 'Silas?'

'Lena!' Silas' voice drifted upwards. He sounded far away.

'Where are you?' Lena called back.

'Down! Please, come quick! I can't move!'

'Stay there, I'm coming!'

Lena reached for her flint and tinder and the small lamp she kept on her.

*No…*

Her lamp wasn't where it should be!

*Alice!*

Lena remembered breaking the lamp when Alice had attacked her outside Nestor's cottage. It looked like she was going have to do this without being able to see.

Lena made her way down the tunnel, feeling her way along and going very slowly in case another part of the floor gave way. As she walked she could hear the scurrying of rats nearby and things sliding over her shoes. She carried on, trying to ignore them

Eventually, Lena came to a fork in the path. Facing the right-hand path Lena felt a soft breeze.

*That must lead up,* she thought.

She turned to the left-hand tunnel and continued her journey. Soon enough it felt like the path was descending. For maybe ten or fifteen minutes more Lena carried on, then, with her next step, the floor vanished. Her hands shot out and she steadied herself. Then she got on her stomach and felt for the edge of the path.

*Steps...*

Lena got back up and slowly, ever so slowly, went down the steps, keeping her hands on the slimy walls to balance herself. One by one, she made her way downwards until she reached the bottom.

'Silas!' Lena called out. 'Can you hear me?'

'This way!' Silas called back. His voice came from ahead and it sounded like he was no longer below her.

'Keep calling out! I'll be there soon!'

Lena followed Silas' voice. The dark pressed on her but she moved forward anyway. Eventually she came to a new tunnel and Silas' voice was coming out of it. She veered to the right. Ahead, she could hear Silas loud and clear.

'Silas?'

'I'm here,' said Silas.

Lena moved down the tunnel slowly until her foot bumped

into something.

'I can't move, Lena,' whispered Silas.

'Are you stuck?'

'No, but I think I've hurt my ankle.'

Lena reached out her hands and felt for Silas. He was sitting huddled on the floor of the tunnel, his legs against his chest and his arms wrapped around his knees. Lena could tell he was panicking; she had seen it happen to people when they returned from a battlefield.

She felt his ankle. It didn't seem broken.

'Come on, Silas, we need to get moving. Remember Berry? We need to find her.'

Lena felt movement in the dark and Silas stood up. She reached out and took his arm in case he slipped.

'I'm up,' said Silas quietly. His voice was less shaky now.

'How's your ankle?'

'I really hurts but I think I can walk if I lean on you.'

Lena put her arm around Silas' waist and he put his over Lena's shoulders.

'The right-hand path above,' said Lena. 'Is that the way out?'

'Yes.'

They made their way through the deep tunnel and then up the stairwell. Silas limped along and occasionally had to grab Lena tightly, but he said nothing and never cried out in pain

When they got to the fork in the tunnel, Lena took them up the path where she had felt the breeze. After five minutes more, Lena saw light coming from the roof ahead. When she got to the light she looked up. It was another grate and she could see the sky above.

Silas cupped his hands and stood under the grate. 'You first,' he said.

'Your ankle?' she asked.

'It's okay, come on.'

Lena put her foot in Silas' hands and pushed herself up to the grate. She then swung the grate open and lifted herself out of the rat-street.

Above ground, Lena found herself in the middle of a flowerbed. Rosebushes covered in wilting red roses surrounded her, reaching just above her head.

'Lena?' called out Silas.

Lena bent down and held out her hands. Silas jumped, grabbed Lena's hands and Lena pulled him up.

Lena could now see Silas clearly; she saw just how bruised and hurt he was.

'Are you okay?' she asked.

'I'll live,' said Silas. 'Nothing's broken at least.'

Lena looked about. 'Where are we?'

'Guillaume Park,' said Silas. He went up to the rosebushes and peered over. Lena joined him.

Beyond, Lena saw a wide expanse of grass with more flowerbeds dotted here and there. Small children were playing games on the grass and people were wandering up and down paths, holding hands and laughing at each other's jokes. In the near distance Lena could see glass palaces full of greenery, and behind the glass buildings was a broad lake with little boats sailing upon it.

Silas went to one corner of the little space in the middle of the flowerbed and got on his hands and knees. He then disappeared into the rosebushes. Lena did the same and they both appeared on the other side. They stood up.

'The first place we'll try is the slave market,' said Silas. 'If Nestor was right and slavers did get her, then that's where they'd sell her.'

They left the park as quickly as they could, although they got quite a few odd looks from the other patrons.

# Chapter Twenty-Six

The slave market was an open space in the eastern quarter of Jultsthorne. Around the edges and in a small circle in the centre were lots of stalls and platforms. Lena felt ill when she saw what was on them: they were selling people. Each stall or platform had men, women and children in cages or held with chains. Meanwhile, visitors to the market were wandering around inspecting those held. Occasionally, Lena saw one of the slaves being taken away by someone after money had changed hands.

'The King lets this happen?' asked Lena.

'I don't think he cares,' Silas replied.

'That's terrible.'

Silas just shrugged.

'Can you see Berry?' said Lena.

Silas looked around. 'No. Let's ask around. Someone must have seen something.'

Lena nodded and they went to the closest stall.

At the stall two men and a young girl were standing in a large cage looking miserable. In front of the cage was a woman calling out numbers while those standing in front of the stall raised their hands.

'The woman is taking bids,' explained Silas. 'The slaves go to whoever will pay the most.'

Lena watched and the bidding soon stopped. The woman pointed at a man near the front and then opened the cage door. The slaves were led out and papers were passed to the man who had bid the most. Once the trade had taken place the crowd moved on while the stall prepared for its next auction.

Silas left Lena, went up to the trader and asked whether she had seen Berry.

'No,' the trader replied. 'But she sounds like she could be at the gladiator stalls. There's not been many fighters coming through the market recently and by the sound of it she'd fetch a pretty penny there.'

'Gladiators?' asked Lena after they had left the trader.

'Jultsthorne has an amphitheatre: The Colosseum,' explained Silas. 'The slaves fight and people watch. It's meant to be fun. Slaves who are good at fighting are called gladiators and they're very valuable. The gladiator stalls are this way.'

The two squires made their way through the market, moving through the churning mass of people.

'Silas?'

The squires spun round to see a plump man coming towards them at speed. He was dressed in a strange shimmering purple robe and a set of gold-rimmed glasses sat on his squat nose.

'Let me handle this,' Silas hissed to Lena. 'Kyle-liar!' he said to the man.

'Silas! I knew it must have been you!' said the man. 'I haven't see you in Jultsthorne for what, five years now?' The man rubbed Silas' hair with a heavily-jewelled hand.

'I left,' said Silas.

'Good for you,' Kyle-liar replied. 'And who's your friend?'

'This is Lena,' Silas replied. 'She's not for sale.'

Kyle-liar looked at Lena closely. 'No, and I can see by the look on her face she's never been to the slaver market before.' He moved between the two squires and put his arms around their shoulders. 'Why don't I buy you a drink and we can catch up.'

Lena was about argue but Silas spoke first.

'It has to be quick,' said Silas. 'But okay.'

'Excellent!' cried Kyle-liar and he bounded ahead.

'What are you doing?' hissed Lena as they followed.

'Trust me,' said Silas. 'He might know something.'

Kyle-liar led the squires to the side of the market where they found a little café with seats and tables scattered around a kiosk. He gestured to the squires to sit and then went to the kiosk to order their drinks.

'Kyle-liar is one of the biggest slavers in the city,' said Silas. 'And spends most of his day here in the market. If Berry were on sale here Kyle-liar would have seen her.'

'Fine,' huffed Lena.

Kyle-liar sat down and his chair creaked. He placed three cups of a green liquid on the table. 'Acenberry juice,' he said with a beaming smile. A waiter then appeared next to him and put a plate of sweets down next to the drinks. 'Eat. Drink!'

'Later,' said Silas. 'I need to ask you something.'

'Anything, Silas!' Kyle-liar replied.

'Have you seen a girl in the market? Thirteen years old. Tall, wiry, got a temper on her.'

Kyle-liar leaned back and rubbed his double chin. 'A girl. A fighter? It doesn't ring any bells. When did she get here?'

'Last night,' Silas replied. 'She was taken from our camp outside the walls. Kidnapped.'

'Kidnapped?' said Kyle-liar. He looked horrified. 'You know we don't allow that here.'

'But it happens anyway,' said Silas. 'Who does it?'

Kyle-liar looked about him and leaned close. He gestured for Silas and Lena to lean in too and they did so.

'Well,' he began. 'You didn't hear it from me but old Gerter has been having troubles. I wouldn't put it past her to start kidnapping people for a bit of extra cash.'

Silas stood up and Lena followed his lead.

'Thanks, Kyle-liar,' said Silas.

Kyle-liar looked at the squires. 'Oh, that's rich! I help you and once you've got what you want, you up and leave. And you haven't touched your drinks!'

'Call it pay-back,' said Silas.

'Ha! I always liked you, Silas. I knew I should have never sold you. Well-' he raised his glass. 'Until we meet again.' He took a long gulp.

Silas and Lena left Kyle-liar to his own company.

'*Sold* you?' said Lena when they were out of ear-shot of Kyle-liar.

'I didn't have parents,' said Silas. 'If you're not an adult here and there's no one to look after you, you're sold to someone who can.'

'That's horrible.'

'Kyle-liar fed me, gave me a place to sleep, taught me to read and count, and then sold me to a rich household. He never hurt me. There are worse lives,' said Silas.

'But you said the Order found you pickpocketing on the streets.'

'Kyle-liar was good to me. The family I was sold to weren't.'

'Oh, sorry.'

'It's okay.'

'Just one more thing. Why is he called "Kyle-liar"?' asked Lena, 'and not just Kyle.'

'Ever heard of the Sins-of-the-Father law?' asked Silas.

'No,' Lena replied.

'In Jultsthorne, if someone is found guilty of a crime, he or she and their children must change their name to reflect the crime. Kyle-liar's dad was caught cheating people out of lots of money so he was called liar and so were his children. It's meant to remind people their crimes will stay with them and their families. Come on, let's find Gerter.'

'Do you know where she is?' asked Lena.

'As long as she hasn't moved since I lived here, yes. She has a warehouse about ten minutes away. Follow me.'

# Chapter Twenty-Seven

Silas led Lena out of the slave market and into a built-up area full of narrow alleys and stray cats. It was much quieter here compared to the hustle and bustle of the market. Silas took Lena down a grim-looking street and at the end of it they came to a large building.

'That was Gerter's warehouse when I lived here,' said Silas. 'I doubt she's moved.'

Light was coming out of a few of the high windows.

'It looks like someone is home,' said Lena. 'So what do we do?'

'Let's see what's going on inside. But we'd best not try the front door.'

They went to each side of the warehouse and then to its rear, but they couldn't find any other way in. All they found was a set of wooden steps that looked like they went to the roof of the warehouse. Unfortunately, most of the steps had rotted away.

'I guess it'll have to be the front door after all,' said Silas. He was about to pull out his sword when Lena grabbed his arm.

Lena stared up at the surrounding buildings. 'Look.'

Silas followed her eyes. 'Oh, okay.'

They moved to the next building along. It was another warehouse but this one was empty. Within, they took a flight of stairs upwards to a door. On the other side of the door was the warehouse roof and the two squires walked across the roof until they could see Gerter's warehouse.

'Looks like we'll have to jump,' said Silas.

Lena didn't hesitate. She moved back, turned, then ran as fast as she could. At the edge of the warehouse she launched herself into the air and came down on the roof of Gerter's warehouse. She rolled to soften the fall and stood up.

'Your turn!' she hissed at Silas across the rooftops.

Silas did the same as Lena, but when he got to the very edge of the building he seemed to falter. He fell forward.

*His ankle!* Thought Lena.

Lena dived forward and managed to grab Silas' hand. Silas looked up at her wide-eyed.

'Got you this time!' gasped Lena.

'Don't let go!'

Lena reached down and grabbed Silas with her other arm. She pulled at him and slowly Silas began to rise. Soon enough, Silas could reach the edge of the building and, with Lena's help, pulled himself onto the roof.

Once he was safe, they both lay back on the roof, panting.

'I forgot about your ankle,' said Lena.

'So did I,' said Silas. 'This hasn't been the best of days, has it?'

From nowhere, Lena found herself almost laughing; she could barely hold it back. They were on the run; most of their friends were either dead or in prison; they had no idea what the future would hold; Berry had been kidnapped; and Silas had nearly died twice in the space of a few hours, both times by falling. Lena wondered if it could get any worse.

She sat up and swallowed her laugh. 'Let's go,' she said, getting up. 'We've got work to do.'

On the roof of Gerter's warehouse they found another door leading inside. Lena went up to it and pushed it open slightly. It looked like no one was on the other side. She opened it a little more and slid through with Silas behind her.

Once they were through the door, Lena and Silas found themselves at the top of an open staircase. Lena went up to the railing and peered over. Below was one big room. In the room were rows of cages, and inside the cages were people. Most of the people were sitting with their backs leaning against the bars. At one end of a row of cages two men were sitting around a table playing cards. *Guards!*

'It doesn't look like Gerter is here,' whispered Silas.

'I can't see Berry either,' said Lena.

'Why don't we ask those two where they are?' Silas looked across the warehouse and Lena followed his gaze. Metal girders crisscrossed the ceiling. 'I think I know how to get them to talk.'

'Go for it,' said Lena.

Silas smiled and jumped up, pulling himself onto the girder closest to him. He stood up and balanced himself. Lena was impressed; she was a better fighter than Silas but she'd never have been able to keep her balance the way Silas was right now.

Lena watched as Silas slowly and silently made his way along the girder until he stood over the two guards. He crouched down, then, seeing his opportunity, grabbed hold of the girder with his hands and dropped.

'Argh!' cried the first guard, who collapsed without a fight as Silas crashed into him.

The second guard was stunned.

'Hi,' said Silas.

The guard looked at his sword lying on the table, but instead of going for it, decided to run. Silas tried to grab him but missed.

'Lena!' Silas called out. He looked down. The guard he had fallen on was groaning and getting up. He couldn't deal with both. 'Stop him!'

Lena was already ahead of Silas. She bolted down the stairs and leapt in front of the second guard.

The second guard twisted his body and slammed into

Lena with his shoulder, sending both of them to the ground. The guard quickly scrambled to his feet and went for the warehouse door but, still on the floor, Lena grabbed his boot and pulled, dragging him back down again.

'Get off me, girl!' the man cried, kicking at Lena and trying to get her to let go.

Lena moved her head and avoided the guard's boot. She then looked down the row of cages. Silas was tying up the first guard as quickly as he could but he couldn't help Lena yet.

The second guard's foot came down again. Lena knocked it aside, grabbed her sword and as she rose drew it from its scabbard on her back. Now, on her feet, she pointed it at the guard's stomach.

'You can stop right there,' said Lena.

The guard slowly got up and raised his hands.

'Move!' said Lena, and she led the second guard to where Silas had tied up the first. Silas tied up the second too.

'Help us!'

Lena spun around. All through the warehouse, those kept in the cages were pushing their hands through the bars, reaching to the squires and begging to be let out.

'They can wait,' said Silas. He looked at the guards. 'This is still Gerter's warehouse isn't it?' he asked the guards. The guards both nodded. 'We're looking for a girl who came here last night. She's about this high and has a mouth on her.'

'She was here,' said the first guard. 'But Gerter took her.'

'Where?' said Silas.

'Colosseum.'

Lena saw Silas' face go white.

Silas looked at Lena. 'We have to go.'

Lena didn't argue. 'What about them?'

Lena looked over at the cages. All the slaves were still pleading for her to free them.

'Keys,' said Silas to the first guard. The guard looked down at his belt to a set of keys. Silas grabbed them and threw them to Lena.

Lena went to the cage closest to her and unlocked the door. The man inside fell out.

'Thank you! Thank you!' cried the man.

Lena gave him the keys. 'Let the others out too,' she said. 'We need to go.'

The man looked at Lena gratefully and went to the cage next to him. He unlocked the cage door and the slave stepped out. By the time the third cage had been opened Lena and Silas had already gone.

# Chapter Twenty-Eight

Lena was shocked; the Twisted Keep was big, but compared to the Colosseum it might have been Nestor's cottage. It was a curved building towering over everything around it. Banners hung from its great arches and all around people were milling about, going in and out of it and buying things from the vendors dotted around the plaza.

'Where do we go?' asked Lena.

'We need to get to where they keep the fighters,' said Silas. grabbing Lena's hand.

Nearby, there was a set of gates built into the side of the Colosseum. Lena watched as the gates opened and a wagon rolled out.

'Here's our chance,' said Silas.

Lena followed his gaze and saw another wagon coming down the street in the other direction.

'Wait for it…go!' hissed Silas.

The squires ran to the closest side of the wagon and ducked down. The wagon turned and went up to the gates; the squires did the same. The gates opened and on the other side of the wagon Lena heard people talking.

'Hello, Pete.' said someone in a gruff voice. Lena guessed it was the gate-keeper. 'Just got the usual?'

'That's right,' said the wagon driver. 'Nice and fresh.'

The wagon started moving again and the squires went with it. The wagon went up to a wooden platform and stopped.

'What do we do now?' whispered Lena.

'Wait,' Silas replied.

Suddenly the floor moved and Lena had to grab the

side of the wagon to keep from falling. The wagon began descending into the depths of the Colosseum. After a short time the lift came to stop. The wagon moved again. As soon as it had cleared the lift the squires split off from it.

'Berry should be somewhere here,' said Silas.

Lena looked around. They were in a vast underground hall full of cages much like the ones in Gerter's warehouse and the market. However, in these cages were not only people. Lions, tigers, and other weird and wonderful creatures were also locked up. It was hot and noisy and Lena wanted to leave as soon as possible.

'What are the animals doing here?' asked Lena.

'The slaves and gladiators fight them,' said Silas. 'Come on, we need to find Berry fast.'

Lena nodded and they started moving through the huge basement. She noticed Silas didn't seem to worry about anyone seeing them now. 'Won't we get caught walking around like this?' asked Lena.

'No. They don't expect anyone to break out,' Silas replied.

They made their way down the aisles, peering into the cages one by one. Suddenly Silas grabbed Lena's arm and pointed to a large man standing by an old woman.

'That's Gerter,' said Silas. 'The man next to her is Douglas, her muscle.'

Lena peered at the pair and saw that Berry was in the cage next them. 'It's her! It's Berry!'

There was a cry through the Colosseum basement.

'Next bout! Get ready! Next bout!'

'What's going on?' asked Lena.

'They're starting the next fight,' said Silas. Lena and Silas could only watch as Berry's cage began to rise.

'She's going to the arena,' Silas replied, his voice shaking.

'Can we stop it?' asked Lena.

'No.'

# Chapter Twenty-Nine

'Good luck, my dear,' said the old woman Berry had learned was called Gerter. Gerter winked at Berry and Berry scowled back.

Douglas, the large man that had grabbed Berry in the Yellowback hills, passed Berry her sword through the bars of the cage, as well as an old, battered shield. 'Be lucky,' said Douglas. 'Fight well.'

Berry's cage rose. She looked around frantically then threw herself at the cage door.

'Fight? Let me out!' she cried. 'What are you doing? Where am I going?'

Above her came a boom as a hatch opened. Weak sunlight poured down from the opening in the ceiling and with the light came the sound of what must be thousands of people cheering.

The cage continued to rise.

Once through the opening, the sides of the cage vanished into the ground and Berry found herself standing in the middle of a huge arena surrounded by a high wall. She looked around open-mouthed. Above the wall were row upon row of seats full of people all cheering. There must have been thousands.

'Move!' hissed Silas.

Lena and Silas turned and ran down a row of cages. They came to a wooden platform with stairs leading up to the ceiling of the basement. Silas went up it and Lena followed. At the top there were wooden hatches. Silas flipped one open and Lena saw the arena. And she saw Berry.

'There's no one else there,' said Lena.

'Not yet,' said Silas. 'Watch.'

'Ladies and Gentlemen!' came a loud voice that carried across the Colosseum. 'We have a new fighter today! Berry the Berserker! And we have Berry's adversary arriving now!'

At the far end of the arena, Berry saw another trapdoor open and a cage appear. Berry's mouth dropped.

'A Flestor!' came the voice. 'Over fifty feet long from tongue to tail, this giant snake from the jungles of Piltz will paralyse its prey with venom and eat them alive! Will Berry the Berzerker defeat the Flestor or will she become its next meal? Place your bets now!'

Lena looked on in horror. 'Silas, we have to help her!'

'There's nothing we can do,' said Silas. 'Not now. Just hope she wins.'

*Come on, Berry,* thought Lena, *you can do this!*

Berry stood where she was and watched as the giant snake moved towards her, its body twisting against the arena floor.

Berry took a couple of steps forward.

The Flestor coiled back and launched itself at Berry. Berry dived to the side, swinging at the Flestor's head, but she missed. She rolled and was back on her feet immediately. The Flestor turned and struck again and Berry only just had time to turn its gaping mouth away with her shield. The sound of it hitting echoed around and the arena and the crowd cheered even louder.

Berry and the Flestor fought each other for short while, but eventually Berry felt her arms starting to tire and she didn't see the Flestor's tail. It swung at Berry's feet and Berry crashed to the ground.

'Ugh!' cried Berry.

The Flestor pounced. It drove forward, raised it head and struck. But with all her strength, Berry lifted her sword at the last possible second. The Flestor couldn't stop; it sank onto the blade with a terrible screech. Still holding the sword, Berry pushed the Flestor's head to one side.

*That was too—*

The Flestor wasn't dead. With the last drop of life it snapped at Berry's leg. One of its fangs went through flesh. Berry cried out and, using her shield, smashed the Flestor's head away, breaking the tooth.

The Flestor stopped moving.

'We have a winner!' cried the announcer. 'Berry the Berserker!'

The crowd in the arena roared. 'Ber-ry! Ber-ry! Ber-ry!' they chanted, waving down at Berry with smiles on their faces.

Berry ignored them and, swaying, made her way to the spot where her cage had appeared. She stood on the spot and the platform lowered. About half way down she collapsed, the Flestor tooth still in her leg.

Lena and Silas flew down the viewing platform and past the cages.

When they got closer to where they had seen Berry in her cage they slowed down. They could see Gerter and Douglas watching Berry's cage come down.

'Look!' hissed Lena.

Berry was lying on the cage floor.

When the cage reached the Colosseum basement again, Gerter and Douglas were waiting for it.

'Get her out of there,' said Gerter.

Douglas took a key from his pocket and unlocked the cage's door. He reached inside and pulled Berry out. He put Berry on her feet, but Berry could barely stay upright.

'She doesn't look in good shape, boss,' said Douglas.

'She's a good fighter,' said Gerter. She took hold of the tooth in Berry's leg and pulled it out.

Berry cried out and Silas had to keep Lena from running

straight to her from their hiding place.

'Too many people here,' hissed Silas. 'We'll never make it out alive.'

'See what Doc Yuletide can do,' said Gerter.

Douglas picked Berry up and cradled her in his arms. He then walked away.

'Let's go,' said Lena.

The squires went down a parallel cage-aisle, keeping Douglas and Berry in sight. At the end of the aisle, Douglas climbed a flight of stairs and at the top, he went up to a door, opened it and stepped out.

Moment later, Lena and Silas came out of the same door and found themselves outside again.

'Why didn't we come in that way?' asked Lena.

Silas let the door close behind him. 'Look.'

Lena saw the outside of the door didn't have a handle. It was impossible to open. 'Oh.'

Lena and Silas looked up to see Douglas walking down the street. They went after him.

# Chapter Thirty

Lena and Silas followed Berry and Douglas to a small house set against the city walls of Jultsthorne. They watched Douglas and Berry enter.

Lena pulled out her sword. 'We go in and get her,' she said.

Silas nodded and drew his own sword. 'Don't hurt anyone if you don't have to. Gerter won't say anything if we just take Berry, but if anyone dies the city watch will be after us.'

Lena nodded. 'Don't worry.' She stood in front of the door to Dr Yuletide's office, kicked it open and dived in.

Within, a man who must have been Dr Yuletide was standing over Berry, who was lying on a stretcher in the middle of a room. Douglas was standing at the far side of the room.

Lena jumped over Berry and before he could do anything, hit Douglas on the side of the head with the hilt of her sword. He went down like a sack of potatoes.

'Who are you?' screamed the doctor. 'What are you doing here?'

'We've come for her,' said Silas, pointing at Berry.

Lena started lifting Berry off the stretcher.

'Lena?' said Berry, her voice weak. 'Is that you?'

'She's that man's slave,' said the Doctor, calmer now knowing the squires didn't look like they were going to hurt him. 'How dare you steal her!'

Silas pointed at Douglas. 'He kidnapped her,' he said.

'Kidnapped?' Dr Yuletide looked disgusted. 'So it *is* true about Gerter.'

Berry was now up and the squires put one of her arms

around each of their shoulders. They were about to leave when the doctor called them back.

'Wait!' Dr Yuletide walked up to them with a vial in his hands. 'Let her drink this. It won't cure her, but it will help her know where she is for a short time.'

'Why should we trust you?' asked Lena.

'Because I believe you about Gerter,' the doctor replied. 'I want to help.'

Silas took the vial, put it to Berry's lips and let her drink. Once it was all gone he handed it back to the doctor.
Berry squirmed and her legs looked like they were working again.

'Thanks,' said Lena.

The doctor nodded. 'Go,' he nodded to Douglas. 'He'll be waking up soon.'

Lena and Silas burst out of Dr Yuletide's office with Berry between them.

'Which way?' asked Lena.

'That way!' Silas replied, pointing to an alley across the street.

The three squires crossed the road, went into the alley and on into the city; Silas giving them directions. Then they halted at a corner.

'Guillaume Park is five minutes that way,' said Silas. 'We're nearly there!'

They were about to step forward when Berry sagged.

'What's wrong?' said Lena.

'I can't do it, Lena,' Berry replied. I'm exhausted. I need to sleep.' Berry's eyes started to close.

'No,' said Lena. 'Stay awake, Berry!'

'No. Leave me,' Berry replied. 'I'll find a way out later.'

'She's losing it,' said Silas. 'We have to move!'

Lena and Silas held onto Berry tightly and were about to take a step forward when a hand grabbed Silas by the arm.

The squires looked up to see a well-dressed man standing in front of them.

'Are you Silas?' asked the man.

'Yes,' said Silas. 'Why?'

'Kyle-liar sent me. Follow me if you want to be safe.'

'No,' said Silas.

The man pointed down the street. Lena and Silas saw Douglas and a group of others running down it.

'Suit yourself,' said the man. He walked ahead briefly and turned down the alley. Silas looked at Lena.

'What do we do?'

Lena looked down the street. Douglas and the rest of Gerter's men were getting closer.

'We don't have any choice,' said Lena. 'Let's go.'

The three squires dived into the alley. They found the man waiting by a door. The man opened the door and ushered the squires inside.

The squires found themselves in what looked like an abandoned room.

'Now what?' asked Lena.

The man went to one wall, took hold of a bookcase standing there and pulled. It swung back with ease.

'This way.'

The next room was much like the first except this one had a trapdoor in the centre of the floor. The man pulled the bookshelf from the other room back to the wall and went over to the trapdoor. He reached down, opened it, and jumped down. The squires went with him, lowering Berry carefully between them.

Below, the squires found themselves in another rat-street. The man lit a torch and led them down the rat-street for maybe fifteen minutes. Above, the squires could hear people walking. They must be under one of the main streets of Jultsthorne.

The man stopped, reached up and pulled down a ladder. He climbed the ladder and pushed open another trapdoor and disappeared.

Going up the ladder, the squires found themselves in a room full of candelabras, soft cushions and golden bowls full of fruit. Against the walls stood a couple of people staring at the floor. In the centre of it all was Kyle-liar.

Ah, Silas and his friends!' said Kyle-liar. 'After we met I saw the fight at the arena.' He pointed to Berry. 'That girl just made me quite a bit of money as everyone else bet on the Flestor, so I think I owe her. I heard about what happened at Dr. Yuletide's too. You'll be safe here. Gerter won't find you.'

'Thanks,' said Lena. She and Silas helped Berry onto a chair. Berry curled up on the chair and groaned. 'But we need to get out of the city as quickly as possible.'

'Not with your friend in that condition you're not,' said Kyle-liar. 'Let's take a look at her shall we?' He signalled two attendants to take Berry.

'We need to go!' said Lena.

'I know, my dear,' said Kyle-liar, 'but let my physicians look after her for an hour or so; you can spare that can't you?'

Lena looked at Berry. Berry looked very ill. 'Okay, but only an hour.'

The attendants lifted Berry carefully and took her out of the room.

'Now,' said Kyle-liar. 'Let's get you rested as well.' He clapped his hands and a set of doors opened. Through the doors came more attendants holding trays of food and drink.

Silas and Lena slumped into two nearby chairs.

'You ran away before you had a chance to eat last time we met,' said Kyle-liar. 'Let's not have that happen again.'

Lena and Silas dived into the food.

Once Silas and Lena were suitably relaxed, Kyle-liar left the squires to doze and went into one of the back rooms of his home. Inside the room were the two attendants and Berry lay on a bed.

Kyle-liar sat on the bed and looked at Berry. 'How is she?' he asked.

'Very ill,' said one. 'We've given her medicine and bandaged the wound properly, but it doesn't look good.'

'Fallengarden...' muttered Berry.

'What was that, child?' asked Kyle-liar.

'Must get to Fallengarden,' said Berry. She then slumped back into sleep.

'Fallengarden?' said Kyle-liar. 'Why would they want to go there? It's just an abandoned castle.'

The attendants looked at Kyle-liar and shrugged.

'Strange...'

Kyle-liar saw Berry was now sleeping properly, so he stood up and left.

Three hours later, Lena woke with a start. She looked around quickly and saw Silas on the chair next to her.

'Silas! Lena called out. She got up and shook Silas by the shoulder.

Silas woke. 'What is it?'

Lena looked out of the window. 'It's getting dark! We need to get back to the others!'

Lena and Silas got up and the doors to the room opened. Kyle-liar came in with a limping Berry and the man who had found the squires on the streets.

'How are you feeling?' asked Lena.

'A little better,' said Berry. 'Thanks for getting me.'

'Don't mention it,' said Lena. She turned to Kyle-liar. 'Thank you for helping us, but we have to go.'

'Of course,' said Kyle-liar. He gestured to the man who had helped them on the street. 'This is Henry. Henry will take you to Guillaume Park and I think from there you will know how to leave our fair city without getting caught.'

'We do,' said Silas. 'And thank you again.'

'Make sure you come back soon!' said Kyle-liar. 'And bring your friends again too. I'm sure you will have many interesting stories to tell.'

Silas nodded and the squires said goodbye.

The squires left Kyle-liar's house and followed Henry through the city to the park. The park was dark now and few people were still wandering through it. After Henry had said his goodbyes, the squires went to the rose garden and then to the rat-street that would get them out of the city.

Lena hoped she would never have to go back to Jultsthorne again.

# Chapter Thirty-One

Lena, Silas and Berry left the rat-street and found themselves outside Jultsthorne's walls again. Wearily, they made their way back to camp and found everyone packing.

'You're just in time,' said Nestor. 'What happened?'

Lena explained all that had passed in Jultsthorne as quickly as she could. Everyone looked at Berry.

'Is she going to be okay?' asked Hounslow, his voice quivering. He looked at Berry. 'Are you going to be okay?'

'We need to get her to Fallengarden,' said Nestor. 'We should find help there.'

He went to his wagon and moved his supplies around. He pushed at Alice too who moved to one side.

'Put her here,' said Nestor. 'I'll watch her.'

Silas and Lena laid Berry on the wagon floor and put a blanket over her.

'Sorry Lena,' said Berry.

'What for?' asked Lena.

'For getting caught.'

'Don't,' said Lena. 'It wasn't your fault. We'll get to Fallengarden. Everything will be all right. I promise.'

Lena took a last look at Berry and turned to the others.

'Let's ride!' she said.

\*\*\*\*

Kyle-liar sat at his desk studying the week's ledgers. Once finished, he sat back in his chair and a contented smile spread across his face. He had made money, got to see Silas once again, and helped someone in need. Definitely a good day.

Kyle-liar felt a breeze on his neck. Strange, he thought

to himself. He stood up and looked around the room. One of the windows was open. He went over to it and closed it, shivering slightly in the autumn wind.

'Kyle-liar,' said a woman's voice.

Kyle-liar spun around. Standing over his desk was a figure dressed entirely in black. Kyle-liar took a few steps closer and saw a masked figure.

'Who are you?' asked Kyle-liar, his anger overtaking his fear. 'What are you doing here?'

The figure flicked over the pages of Kyle-liar's ledger.

'This makes for some interesting reading,' said the figure. 'I imagine you would want this kept out of certain hands.'

'Get out!' cried Kyle-liar.

The figure turned and flew across the room. Before Kyle-liar had a chance to relax the woman in black was standing over him. Kyle-liar was terrified.

'Sit down,' said the figure, and Kyle-liar did so.

'What do you want?' asked Kyle-liar.

'I heard reports about three children causing a lot of problems in Jultsthorne,' said the woman. 'A warehouse broken into; a commotion at Dr. Yuletide's office; a chase through the streets; then they disappeared apparently. In the company of one of your employees.'

'I don't know what you're talking about.'

The figure stepped closer and drew a small crossbow from the folds of her cloak. She pointed it at Kyle-liar.

'I don't have time for this,' said the figure. 'What happened to them?'

Kyle-liar told the figure all that had happened.

'Good,' said the figure. 'Now, where are they going?'

'Fallengarden,' said Kyle-liar. He slumped in his chair. 'They're going to Fallengarden.'

The figure went to the window and climbed out.

'I'm sorry, Silas,' said Kyle-liar to himself. 'I'm so sorry.'

# Chapter Thirty-Two

The squires crested a hill and Fallengarden came into view just as the sun was setting. The old, abandoned castle sat on a cliff edge; almost a silhouette against the angry red dusk sky. It looked like it had seen better days. Its walls sagged as if they were about to come crashing down, and many of its towers appeared to have already succumbed to time and neglect. Lena imagined a strong gust of wind would cause the whole place to collapse.

'That's where we'll be safe?' she asked.

'Aye,' said Nestor. 'Don't let her looks deceive you.'

They made their way down the hill and up the bare ground to the ivy-covered gatehouse of Fallengarden. When they arrived they saw the gates had gone long ago. All that was left was a gaping hole.

Nestor took the lead. 'This way,' he said, geeing the horse into Fallengarden's courtyard.

The courtyard itself was dark, overgrown and utterly deserted; no light came from any of the windows of the castle's keep either.

'No one's home,' said Hounslow.

Lena felt her stomach churn. Had their journey been for nothing? No one lived here; it was obvious. Fallengarden was just an empty ruin. What would they do now?

Nestor rode his wagon to the middle of the courtyard and stopped. He looked around for a time; squinting at the parapets, battlements and windows.

'What are you doing?' asked Lena.

Nestor ignored Lena's question. Instead, he called out:

'We are here, brothers and sisters!'

Suddenly the ground shook. Lena watched open-mouthed as the far section of the courtyard floor rose into the air. Pillars with lit torches lifted the courtyard floor high off the ground. Underneath, another platform appeared. Knights wearing Order armour were standing on it.

'Nestor,' said the closest knight. 'It's good to see you.' There was a hiss and the knight removed their helmet. Underneath was a woman with long auburn hair, a sharp nose, and piercing green eyes.

'Madeleine,' said Nestor. 'It's good to see you too. We have a great deal to talk about.'

The knight and Nestor embraced.

'I assumed as much,' said the knight, now serious. 'We heard about the attack on the Twisted Keep only a few days ago.' The knight then looked at the squires. 'And who might they be?'

'Survivors from the Twisted Keep,' said Nestor. He turned to the squires. 'This is Madeleine Loquanto, Grandmaster of the Order of the Embers.'

Grandmaster Madeleine bowed. 'It is good to meet you all and welcome to Fallengarden. Please, come with me.'

'Order of the Embers?' asked Lena. 'What's that?'

'Let us talk below,' said Nestor. 'You'll get better answers to your questions there.'

Nestor moved his wagon onto the platform and the squires joined him. There was a rumbling and the platform began to descend again.

# Chapter Thirty-Three

It was late at night when Sir Poland received a knock on his cell door. He woke with a start.

'Sir Poland!' came a woman's voice from the other side of the door. 'Please! Wake up!'

'I'm awake,' Sir Poland replied. He stood up and went to the door. The viewing shutter was closed and there was no way to open it from inside the cell. He couldn't see who was speaking.

'I'm here to help,' said the voice. 'It's time to get you out of here.'

'Who are you?' said Sir Poland.

There was a click and the cell door swung open. Sir Poland didn't recognise the woman on the other side.

'My name is Yvette,' said the woman. 'There's no time to talk. Come with me.'

Yvette led Sir Poland through the corridors of Casenberg dungeon, past occupied and empty cells, until they reached a dark dead end. She searched the wall until something clicked and a section of it swung away, revealing a stairwell.

'This way,' said Yvette.

Sir Poland followed Yvette into the cobweb-covered stairwell. At the top, Yvette pushed at a door and it swung outwards. On the side of the door was an ordinary-looking front room.

'Where is everyone else?' asked Sir Poland, looking around. 'Was I the first?'

'I could only get you,' Yvette replied. 'The others must stay where they are.'

'We must go back!' cried Sir Poland. 'I cannot leave them!'

'We can't,' said Yvette. 'It was hard enough getting you out! Every cell has a different key and the more people we try to release the more likely someone will spot what we are doing.'

Sir Poland knew she was right. 'Why are you doing this?' he asked. 'Who are you?'

'I worked for Erin-'

Yvette saw Sir Poland tense.

'But not any more! I don't like what she and the King are doing.'

'You are risking a great deal,' said Sir Poland. 'Thank you.'

'We need to get out of the city. I know things about Erin and the King ,' said Yvette. 'I can help you fight back.'

'I think that can be arranged,' said Sir Poland. 'What do we do now?'

'First we get out of the city,' said Yvette. 'Then we go to a place where I have horses and supplies. After that, it's up to you. But first...' she looked Sir Poland up and down. 'You'll need to look a bit more appropriate.' There was a bag on a chair nearby. She picked it up and threw it to Sir Poland. 'These should fit.'

It was still dark outside when Sir Poland and Yvette stepped out onto the street. Casenberg was quiet at this time of night. Only a few lights shone out from windows and no one was outside.

'We'll leave by the main gate,' said Yvette. 'This way.'

They walked through Casenberg as calmly as possible, passing only a few people and night-watchmen doing their rounds.

Sir Poland studied the city as they walked through it. Casenberg was still a beautiful place despite the corruption at its heart. Sir Poland had visited the city when he became Knight-Commander of the Order of the Furnace and he had been astonished at the city's elegance back then. He had been presented to the King, whose disease had yet to fully take hold by then. However, as the King gave Sir Poland his badge of office, Sir Poland remembered seeing the sickness in the King's eyes and on the King's skin.

After what seemed like a very long, tense time, Sir Poland and Yvette came to the main gate of Casenberg. Only a few guards were on duty at this time of night and they looked tired and bored.

'Let me handle this,' said Yvette. She walked up to the gate. Sir Poland stayed with her.

'Stop!' cried one of the guards. He looked at both Yvette and Sir Poland suspiciously. 'Papers?'

Yvette handed the man a document. The man looked at it briefly and quickly returned it. He turned to the other guards. 'Open the gate!'

Casenberg's main gate opened with a loud groan.

'Thank you, Captain,' said Yvette.

'Ma'am,' said the Captain, touching the tip of his helmet. He looked at Sir Poland. 'Sir.'

Sir Poland nodded to the guard and he and Yvette stepped onto the Hulit causeway, a long stone bridge that spanned a ravine many hundreds of feet deep. The gate clanged shut behind them.

'That was very easy,' said Sir Poland suspiciously.

'Working for Erin has its benefits,' Yvette replied. 'Very few people either ask questions or delay me. It looks like they don't know you've escaped yet either, so they're not looking for you. Let's go, we have a lot of ground to cover before morning.'

# Chapter Thirty-Four

Lena felt the platform that was taking them under Fallengarden castle come to a halt. She looked around and found herself in a large, arched hall lit with iron chandeliers that hung from the ceiling. At the other end of the hall was a broad fireplace taking up most of the far wall and between Lena and the fireplace was a crowd of people. The crowd stood around the platform. There were perhaps a few hundred, if not more. Most looked like knights and were looking at the squires curiously.

'These are the survivors of the Twisted Keep,' announced Grandmaster Madeleine in a loud voice. 'Welcome them as friends. They have come very far and have endured much to be here. Show them the hospitality of the Order of the Embers.'

The crowd cheered the squires as if they were a victorious army home from a long war. Lena was taken aback.

Grandmaster Madeleine continued: 'As you all know, we have been dealt a harsh blow with the fall of the Twisted Keep. We have lost friends and we have our own people in prison in the depths of Casenberg. But this will change! The kingdom will rise again. We will be free!'

The crowd cheered again. Some of those at the front of the crowd came up to the squires to greet them and lead them off the platform.

Once the crowd started to disperse, Nestor spoke. 'Madeleine, we have an injured knight with us.'

Nestor took Grandmaster Madeleine to the back of his cart, showed her Berry and explained what had happened.

Grandmaster Madeleine called a couple of attendants over. 'Take her to the infirmary,' she commanded. 'She has been bitten by a Flestor. See what the medics can do.'

As Berry was being moved, Alice stirred. The attendants jumped back in fear as Alice stepped off Nestor's wagon. Some of the knights even drew their weapons.

Nestor stepped between the knights and Alice. 'She's with us!' he said, using his most charming grin. 'Don't be afraid.'

The knights watched as Alice nuzzled against Nestor.

'See?' said Nestor. 'No danger here.'

The knights put their swords away but still watched Alice cautiously.

'She still looks like she's just been made,' said Grandmaster Madeleine, patting Alice on the head. 'I haven't seen her in years.'

'I try to look after her as best I can,' said Nestor. He turned serious. 'Madeleine, can you take me to Oliguer?'

'Of course,' replied the Grandmaster. 'We are very glad you are here. I, and Oliguer, desperately need your help.'

Silas poked Lena. 'Who's Oliguer?'

'No idea,' Lena replied.

Grandmaster Madeleine led Nestor and the squires to a set of doors leading off the great hall. They went through it, down a corridor, and found themselves in front of a large set of double-doors built into the stone. Grandmaster Madeleine pushed them open.

'This is where Oliguer rests,' said the Grandmaster.

On the other side of the double-doors was a massive, curved chamber. Lena whistled in surprise. Grandmaster Madeleine went to the wall on one side of the double-doors and pulled at a lever. The chamber flooded with light as lanterns set high in the ceiling lit themselves.

Now she could see clearly, Lena guessed there must be at least five or six hundred feet between the entrance of the room and the far wall. In the centre of the room Lena saw a huge machine. It was curled up, with what appeared to be massive, leathery wings covering most of its body. It wasn't moving.

'What is *that?*' said Hounslow.

'That is Oliguer,' said Grandmaster Madeleine. 'One of the greatest soul-machines ever built.'

'It's not moving,' said Lena.

'Oliguer went to sleep many years ago once the Great Wars ended and the Ancient Ones had been driven back into the sea,' explained the Grandmaster. 'Oliguer was too powerful to remain active but, if ever something happened that needed his might, he would be here for us to call upon.'

'So why aren't we waking him up?' asked Lena.

'We tried,' the Grandmaster replied. 'But something is wrong. Nothing will get him to stir. That is why Nestor is here.'

Nestor walked up to Oliguer and looked him over while rubbing his chin.

'I'll need time to examine him,' he said, 'and I'll need my tools from my wagon.'

'As you wish,' Madeleine replied.

'Can I help?' said Hounslow.

Grandmaster Madeleine looked to Nestor.

'Fine with me,' said Nestor. 'Maybe you'll learn something.'

Madeleine turned to Lena and the other squires. 'I imagine you have a lot of questions, and you look like you could do with some hot food inside you. Come with me. We have bunks and food waiting and we can talk then.'

# Chapter Thirty-Five

Erin sat at her candle-lit desk in her home in the wealthiest district of Casenberg. In front of her were numerous papers; reports about the empire and its enemies. She liked to know everything that was going on: she had spies in every city and town in Eltsvine as well as in most of the courts in the kingdoms and lands beyond Eltsvine's borders. Knowledge is power after all.

There was a slight gust of wind. Erin put down the piece of paper in her hand and placed a paperweight on the reports. Her Jasareen spies and assassins were possibly the best in the world (she had trained most of them herself), but their desire to use windows rather than the front door could be a pain.

'Hello Lucy,' said Erin to a shadow in the corner of the room. 'What have we learned? Do we know where the children are?'

A figure all in black came out of the shadow and bowed low.

'They have gone Fallengarden, my lady,' replied Lucy.

'Fallengarden?' Erin replied. 'An abandoned castle in the east of the Empire, on the coast of the Olive Ocean. Why would they have gone there?'

'It is unclear,' Lucy replied. 'I only know that is where they are going, not why.'

Erin pondered for a time. 'Who do we have in the area?'

'The Third Army can be at Fallengarden in a week,' Lucy replied. 'The rest are on our borders and miles away.'

'Send the Third Army then. They have Powder don't they?'

'Yes, but we're still not finished testing it. It is still very unstable.'

'I want it used,' said Erin. 'Show everyone the Order are not the only ones with interesting toys.'

'But they are only a few children,' said Lucy.

'They are knights in what was the best fighting force the world has ever known. And as I recall two of them left you a little bruised and battered at the Twisted Keep.'

'As you say, my lady.'

'Also,' continued Erin. 'Tell the general of the third army to be on her guard. Sir Poland wouldn't have just sent them to an abandoned castle for no reason.'

'Yes, my lady.'

'You may go.'

Lucy stepped back into the shadows and disappeared.

Suddenly there was knock on the door to Erin's study.

'What now?' Erin muttered to herself. 'There is no peace. Enter!'

The study door opened and Erin's butler, Greaves, appeared.

'A runner is at the door,' said Greaves. 'He is from the Captain of the Palace Guard. The Captain has requested your presence. It sounds very serious, my lady.'

'About time. Thank you, Greaves,' said Erin. She stood up, walked out of her room and to the front door of her home. She found the messenger waiting for her.

'Take me to the Captain,' said Erin.

The messenger led Erin to the Palace where they were ushered in immediately. Once inside the grand foyer, Erin saw the Captain of the guard. He rushed up to her. The Captain looked deeply worried.

'My lady,' said the Captain. 'Something terrible has happened. The King ...'

Erin raised her hand and shushed the Captain. 'Not here. People can overhear. Take me to the royal chambers.'

The Captain led Erin through the palace to the golden elevator. They entered and it took them to the royal apartment. When they arrived, Erin saw a group of guards standing outside. They were as white as sheets; some were shaking.

Erin and the Captain entered the apartment and immediately covered their mouths. The smell was even worse than usual.

'He's in the bedroom, my lady,' said the Captain.

Erin followed the Captain into the royal bed chamber. Lying on the bed was the King : dead.

'What happened?' asked Erin.

'The guards brought him his supper and found him like this,' said the Captain. 'There's also something else.'

'Go on,' said Erin.

'Sir Poland, my lady. He has escaped.' The Captain winced.

'So, Sir Poland has done this,' said Erin calmly.

'Well, there's no proof...' began the Captain. Erin held up her hand to the Captain. 'It is a certainty,' she said. 'This looks like it happened only a few hours ago too. Send out your soldiers and put word out that Sir Poland is to be found. Alive preferably.'

The Captain saluted. 'Yes, my lady,' he said. Then he ran out of the room.

Erin looked at the King and smiled. It was too perfect.

# Chapter Thirty-Six

Lena and the squires sat at a long table in the underground cloister where they had been given bunks. Grandmaster Madeleine had taken them to the cloister after they had seen Oliguer. The journey had given Lena a chance to understand just how big Fallengarden really was. Under the ruins of the castle, it was the same size as the Twisted Keep if not bigger. There were libraries, training rooms, stables, armouries and storerooms all buried in the cliff-face.

Lena looked at all the food that had been prepared for the squires: steaming roast potatoes, glistening chicken legs, glazed carrots and peas, and succulent slices of beef.

'Eat!' cried Madeleine.

The squires dived into the food.

When she was feeling better, Lena turned to Madeleine.

'Who *are* you?' she asked.

'We are the Order of the Embers,' said Grandmaster Madeleine. 'We are a part of the Order of the Furnace, but we don't work the same way you do.'

'I've never heard of you,' said Silas.

'Good!' said Madeleine. 'That means we're doing our job!'

'What do you do?' asked Lena.

'We do things that the Order of the Furnace cannot. We stay in the shadows and gather information in countries where the Order of the Furnace can't tread. Think of it this way: the Order of the Furnace protects the kingdom from obvious threats while the Order of the Embers protects it from the less obvious ones. We are two sides of the same coin.'

'Why weren't we told about you?' asked Lena.

'The fewer people that know about us the better. Not even the King knows we exist, even though we have been fighting for him for just as long as the Order of the Furnace.'

'There's not many of you,' said Silas. 'Do you think you can fight all the royal armies?'

The Grandmaster looked at Silas. 'Sadly, no. The Order of the Embers can do many things, but against the kingdom itself we would be likely to fail.'

Lena stared at the Grandmaster. 'We have come all this way and you can do nothing? Why did we come here?'

'Do not jump to conclusions, Lena. I know about you from Sir Poland and he would be very disappointed to hear you thinking that way.'

Lena shuffled in her seat.

'Right now,' continued Grandmaster Madeleine, 'the Order of the Embers could not take on the kingdom, but then neither could the Order of the Furnace if it was on its own. Eltsvine is just too big. It can raise thousands of soldiers and would beat both the Order of the Furnace and the Order of the Embers simply on numbers alone.'

'So what can we do?' asked Lena.

'What do you think?' asked Grandmaster Madeleine. 'Sir Poland has trained you. What does your training say?'
Lena thought about it.

'Not have an open battle,' she said eventually. 'At least not at the start.'

'Good,' said Madeleine. 'So what do we do instead?'

Lena remembered the siege of Castle Winlow and she remembered what the Duke had said. 'We find allies. There are a lot of people unhappy with the King . If we all come together...'

'Exactly,' said the Grandmaster. 'As soon as we learned about what had happened at the Twisted Keep we sent out messengers to those who have power in the empire but dislike the King : dukes and counts who are sick of the King's demands and those who have lost their homes. There are a lot of people in the kingdom who want to see the King fall and his wars to come to an end.'

'So we're going to have a war to stop the wars?' asked Silas.

'Unfortunately, that appears to be the only way,' Grandmaster Madeleine replied.

'What about Oliguer? What can it do?' asked Lena.

'He,' not 'it!' Oliguer is part of the plan,' said the Grandmaster. 'He is very powerful and can turn the tide of any battle, but a war is rarely fought one battle at a time and we have to be careful with Oliguer. Right now, we need him just to survive, but there is a danger he could drive potential allies away out of fear. It is a difficult path we walk.'

'I understand,' said Lena. 'What's the plan now?'

'We wait,' said the Grandmaster. 'No one knows we are here. Oliguer is not ready and we have not heard back from our potential allies. There is little more we can do until then.'

'But what about those taken by Erin?' said Silas. 'We can't leave them.'

'We know they are being held in the dungeons of Casenberg,' the Grandmaster replied. 'We have agents in the city but so far they have been unable to get to the dungeons.'

Lena nodded and understood. She might not see the knights of the Order taken at the Twisted Keep ever again.

The squires finished their meal in silence. Once it came to an end they went their separate ways. Some went to rest in their bunks, others went to explore and some went to train.

Lena and Silas approached Grandmaster Madeleine.

'Can we see Berry?' asked Lena.

'Of course,' said the Grandmaster. 'This way.'

The Grandmaster stood up from the table and led Lena and Silas to the infirmary.

# Chapter Thirty-Seven

Lena and Silas found the infirmary near the cloister. It was a broad room full of beds with a row of high windows. Berry was in one of the beds. A medic stood over her.

Lena, Silas and the Grandmaster walked up to Berry's bed. 'This is Dr. Yelen,' said Grandmaster Madeleine.

Dr. Yelen looked up from Berry and greeted the Grandmaster and the squires. He was an old man with a bald head, soft, sad eyes, and a grey drooping moustache.

'Good to meet you,' he said.

'How is she?' asked Lena. She looked down at Berry. Berry's eyes were closed and she looked ever so pale.

'Your friend is not so good,' Dr. Yelen replied. 'The Flestor that bit her managed to get a lot of its poison into her system. It's a wonder she's still alive.'

'What will happen to her?' asked Lena.

The medic looked grave.

'I don't know,' he said. 'All we can do now is wait and see. But you may need to prepare yourself for the worst.'

Berry was covered in sweat and squirmed as if she couldn't get comfortable no matter how hard she tried.

'Can she hear us?' asked Silas.

'I don't think so,' said the medic.

Lena lent over Berry. 'Stay strong, Berry. You can get through this,' Lena felt a terrible lump in her throat. 'You defeated the Flestor and you got out of Jultsthorne. You've won more fights than any of us. You can do this!'

The Grandmaster, Silas and Lena left Dr. Yelen to continue his work.

# Chapter Thirty-Eight

So far on their journey Sir Poland and Yvette had been lucky and managed to get away from Casenberg without anyone stopping them.

When they reached a crossroads a few miles away from Casenberg, Yvette stopped. They were in a wooded area and it was still very dark. The trees cast long shadows across the road in the moonlight and what they guessed were animal noises nearby put them on their guard.

'There's a cabin not far from here,' said Yvette. 'We should go there to eat and rest for a time.'

'Are we far enough away from Casenberg?' asked Sir Poland.

'The cabin is well hidden and they won't know you're missing until morning,' Yvette replied.

They left the road and made their way through the woods. It was hard going; they couldn't risk lighting torches in case anyone saw them.

Eventually, they came out next to a stream and they followed it. About an hour later, they came to a small hut. Yvette unlocked the door and they went inside.

'No fires, just in case,' said Yvette. She went over to a cupboard, opened it and passed thick blankets to Sir Poland. 'Here, you can use these to keep warm.'

Sir Poland thanked Yvette and wrapped the blankets around himself.

Yvette then gave Sir Poland some dried meat, bread and a bottle full of water. He took a bite from the meat and bread and swallowed a gulp of the water.

'Thank you for all your help,' said Sir Poland.

'I had to do it,' said Yvette. 'I knew the King was mad, but when he attacked the Twisted Keep and brought you to Casenberg, that was the final straw. I hope what I know will help. What do you intend to do now?'

'The Order has friends,' Sir Poland replied. 'I can't tell you more, but we shall go to them.'

Sir Poland's eyes started to get heavy. 'Sleep,' said Yvette. 'I'll wake you at dawn and we can move on then'

Sir Poland lay down and pulled the thick blanket over him.

Hours later, Sir Poland woke to Yvette shaking his shoulder.

'It's morning,' said Yvette.

Sir Poland pulled the blankets off him and rose. 'You said something about horses,' he said.

'This way.' Yvette led Sir Poland out of the hut. A few metres away were two horses tied to a tree with travel packs attached to their saddles. She untied one of the horses and handed the reins to Sir Poland.

'This one is yours,' said Yvette. 'The packs have a tent, food, and everything we'll need for our journey. You'll find a sword there too.'

'Excellent,' said Sir Poland. 'You've prepared very well.' He patted the horse's neck and swung himself into its saddle. Yvette mounted her horse too.

'Which way?' said Yvette.

'East,' said Sir Poland. 'We head East.' Sir Poland looked towards the Sun. 'This way.'

The made their way through the forest slowly and carefully. It was a treacherous journey but they couldn't risk the roads this close to Casenberg. Around this time, Sir Poland was normally woken in his cell by whichever guard was on duty to ensure he was still there. Today, the guard would be in for a surprise.

The day passed, and then another and another. The woods ended, and Sir Poland and Yvette found themselves in farmland.

'We're close now,' said Sir Poland.

Ahead, was a barn. Sir Poland and Yvette rode up to it and opened its doors. It was empty.

'What do we do now?' said Yvette.

'We wait,' Sir Poland replied.

A day later, Sir Poland woke to the barn door creaking open. Sir Poland and Yvette grabbed their weapons and prepared themselves.

'Who goes there?' Sir Poland called out.

'Embers of the fire,' came a voice.

'Borne of the furnace,' Sir Poland called back.

'Shall never perish,' said the voice.

The door opened and a man and woman in armour stepped inside the barn.

'Sir Poland?' said the man. 'We're here to help.'

Sir Poland laughed. 'Thank the Gods you're here!' he cried. 'I was concerned that I'd got the wrong barn!'

Yvette eyed the two soldiers suspiciously. 'Who are they?' she asked.

'For now, it's best you don't know,' Sir Poland replied. 'But they will make our journey a lot easier.'

# Chapter Thirty-Nine

A week passed under the ruins of Fallengarden, then two. Lena, the squires and Hounslow trained, studied and helped the Order of the Embers while they waited for Nestor to finish his work and to hear back from the messengers sent out across the empire.

It was a frustrating time for Lena. She badly wanted to do something; anything would do that didn't involve being kept in the depths of Fallengarden and would help those trapped in Casenberg. But she knew, right now, waiting was best.

One morning, Lena stood in a training circle and waited for Silas to strike. His blade came forward and Lena knocked it aside. They carried on, their swords crashing into one another until they were both exhausted.

'Good,' said Lena. 'You're getting better.'

'I'm not as good as Berry though,' said Silas. 'You could have had me three times as far as I could tell.'

'Five,' Lena replied.

Silas mock-sneered and went over to the weapons rack. He was about to hang his weapon when a young knight burst into the training room.

'Soldiers!' He cried.

'What?' said Lena. 'Where?'

'Outside!' replied the knight. He ran out of the room and into the rest of the Fallengarden. Lena could hear his voice echoing down the corridors.

'There can't be,' said Lena. 'No one knows anyone is here.'

'We should check this out,' said Silas.

Lena nodded and they made their way out of the training

rooms and up a stairwell that would take them to the towers and battlements of Fallengarden. On the stairs were other knights all keen to see what was going on too.

At the top of the stairwell was a trapdoor. Knights were going through it and Lena and Silas had to wait their turn. Finally, they went through the trapdoor and found themselves on a parapet that overlooked the plain in front of Fallengarden. All along the parapet, knights were looking out at the scene. Lena and Silas joined them.

'It's impossible...' said Silas. 'How could they have known we are here?'

Coming down the hillside were columns of soldiers. There must have been hundreds, both on foot and on horseback. Behind the soldiers were siege weapons. They were nowhere near as impressive as the Order's Bulls, Ballistae Hounds and Auto-Trebuchets, but they could do still do the job if need be. The army stopped a good distance from Fallengarden and began to dig in.

'It's the Royal Army,' said Lena.

'How did they find us?' asked Silas.

'I have no idea.'

Once the army had stopped, the squires watched as a single rider came towards Fallengarden. When the rider was closer, he stopped and spoke.

'Squires of the Order of the Furnace,' the rider cried, sounding annoyed more than anything else. 'We are here in the name of King Claudio. Surrender and we will let you live.'

Everyone on the battlement remained silent and ducked down out of sight.

'Look,' said the rider. 'We know you're here. We've been ordered to bring the castle down if you don't surrender. We don't want to, but if you don't come out we'll bury you.' The rider pointed at siege weapons. 'Do you see those? We're not kidding around here.'

Lena felt a tap on her shoulder. She turned and saw Grandmaster Madeleine.

'They are here for you,' said the Grandmaster. 'How did they know where to look?'

'I don't know!' hissed Lena. 'I haven't told anyone and me, Silas and Berry haven't met anyone since we found Nestor and were told we were coming here.'

'Were you separated at any point?' said the Grandmaster.

Lena and Silas went white.

'What is it?' asked Grandmaster Madeleine. 'Speak!'

'When Berry got injured,' said Lena. 'She might have said something to someone. She was alone with a few people then.'

'We may be lucky,' said Grandmaster Madeleine. 'All they know is you aimed to come here. They may think you've already left.'

As if the rider below had heard Madeleine, he called out: 'We've been ordered to tear this place down anyway so it doesn't matter if you are here or not! Is anyone there? Or am I just talking to myself? This is utterly ridiculous!'

'It looks like the King has forced our hand,' said the Grandmaster. She stood over the battlements and spoke to the rider. 'You'll find more than squires here, sir!'

'The rider looked at Madeleine, dumb-founded. 'Who are *you?*' he called back.

'I am Grandmaster Madeleine,' replied the Grandmaster. 'And these are my knights. Arise!'

Lena watched as all along the battlements and in the towers the Order of the Embers showed themselves. It was a mighty sight.

The rider went wide-eyed. He then turned and rode as fast as he could back to the Royal Army. 'There's an army here!' Lena heard the rider cry. 'There's a whole army!'

Lena looked at the Grandmaster. 'I'm sorry we brought

them here,' she said.

'It couldn't be helped,' said Madeleine. She looked around the battlements. 'Knights, our plans have changed. Ready defences!'

'What defences?' said Silas to Lena. 'We walked straight into Fallengarden when we got here.'

'Only because we let you,' Madeleine replied, overhearing the squires' conversation. 'Watch.'

Moments later, there was a deep rumbling sound. Lena looked down at Fallengarden's gatehouse and saw the ground open up. A huge block of stone rose, blocking Fallengarden's entrance more completely than any gate could.

More noises echoed around the castle. Towers appeared from nowhere and walls that Lena had thought were about to fall looked a great deal stronger. On top of the towers and walls Lena saw ballistae and catapults unfold themselves and take aim. In front of Fallengarden, longs spikes rose out of the ground at forty-five degrees and a moat uncovered itself.

Fallengarden was now a fortress.

'Inside,' ordered Madeleine. 'We need to make preparations.'

# Chapter Forty

Madeleine stood in the centre of the great hall and Lena and Silas stood close by. The hall was now full, almost everyone in the Order of the Embers could be seen as well as Lena's squires.

Above, Lena heard the dull thud of the Royal Army's catapults pummelling Fallengarden's walls and the Order's own weapons firing back. Dust drifted down from the ceiling occasionally.

'The King knows we are here,' Madeleine announced. 'We cannot hide in the depths of Fallengarden and we may need to meet this army on the battlefield. This could be the first step in retaking the kingdom, brothers and sisters, let's make it count!'

The hall erupted in cheers.

'For the Order!' they cried. 'For the Empire!'

The knights of the Order of the Embers dispersed. Lena's squires went with them to help where they could.

Lena then saw Nestor approach Madeleine.

'I heard what's happened,' said Nestor. 'This throws a spanner in the works somewhat.'

'Yes and no,' Madeleine replied. 'If we defeat them here it could have an important effect on those looking to rebel against the King . They may see a victory here as a reason to join us.'

'It's risky, Madeleine,' said Nestor.

'We don't have any choice,' the Grandmaster replied. 'What is happening with Oliguer?'

'I have replaced a few of Oliguer's parts that looked a little worn, but I think I know now what the real problem is,' said Nestor.

'And that is?' asked the Grandmaster.

'Oliguer is gone.'

'What?'

'The spirit of Oliguer is no longer there. Oliguer didn't go to sleep Madeleine, he's passed on to the other side. That machine is just that: a machine only.'

'What can we do?' asked Grandmaster Madeleine. 'Without Oliguer we have little chance of success.'

'The machine needs a new soul,' said Nestor quietly.

Madeleine was quiet for a moment. 'But that means…'

'We need a sacrifice,' said Nestor.

'I don't want to hear this, Nestor.'

'Maybe not, but this is the situation. It must be human too. Any animal soul would go mad inside Oliguer's body. It would be too alien for it.'

'I will think of some names,' said the Grandmaster. 'I loathe to lose anyone but if that is what is needed.'

'They need to be strong-willed,' said Nestor. 'And loyal.'

Lena spoke up. 'There's Berry,' she said, but the Grandmaster and Nestor continued speaking only to one another. 'I said: there's Berry!'

'What's that, girl?' said the Grandmaster.

'What are you doing, Lena?' hissed Silas.

Lena ignored Silas. 'Berry could do it. I visit her every day but she's not getting better, and Dr. Yelen doesn't even pretend she will any more. We're just waiting for the poison to take her. I don't want to do it, but…'

The Grandmaster looked at Nestor. 'Do you think she would be suitable?'

Nestor rubbed his chin. 'Maybe. She's brave and bright enough, that's for certain. But could she cope with the change? I don't know. The poison would have weakened her body too. The Taking is a dangerous process and it may be too much even for her.

'She can do it,' said Lena.

Grandmaster Madeleine gazed at Lena carefully. 'Do it, Nestor,' said Madeleine. 'Berry is my choice.'

Nestor nodded. 'I'll begin straight away.'

'Wait,' said Silas. 'Is this right? Can we do this to Berry?'

Lena looked at Silas. 'Yes, it is and we must. I don't like it either, Silas, but could you ask anyone here to take her place?'

Silas looked around the great hall, at the knights and squires preparing themselves for battle. He turned back to Lena. 'As you command.'

Lena turned to Nestor 'Can we say goodbye first?'

'Of course,' Nestor replied.

# Chapter Forty-One

Lena looked down at Berry in her hospital bed. Nestor stood next to her, as did Silas. Berry looked very ill. Her skin looked as if was about to fall from her body and her hair was thin and shining with sweat. For the past few days, Lena had noticed Berry's eyelids didn't even flicker any more either.

'Berry?' said Lena softly. 'I don't know if you can hear me but we need your help once again.'

Berry looked so small in the hospital bed. So fragile.

'We are in danger,' explained Lena. 'There is an army above us that wants us dead. We are trapped and cannot escape. We will fight them, but we might not win and all this would have been for nothing. You can make it so we can survive today and maybe we can even strike back and take back our home.' Lena lent closer and held one of Berry's hands and turned to Nestor. 'Will she know what is happening?'

'I don't know,' said Nestor. 'It has been many years since a person was placed inside a machine. It was forbidden all that time.'

'Will she remember us?' asked Silas.

'I don't know.'

Nestor reached down and picked Berry up in his arms. He turned to Lena and Silas. 'It's probably best you don't see what happens next,' said Nestor. 'I won't hurt her but it is not pleasant to watch.'

Lena and Silas watched Nestor take Berry to Oliguer's lair with tears in their eyes.

'I hope this works,' said Silas.

'So do I,' Lena replied.

# Chapter Forty-Two

Lena and Silas made their way back to the great hall. They walked back in silence. Neither could even meet the other's eye.

Once they arrived in the great hall Grandmaster Madeleine came over to them.

'Lena,' said the Grandmaster. 'Come with me. Silas you can come too. I have something that might lighten your mood.'

Grandmaster Madeleine led Lena and Silas through the tunnels of Fallengarden until they came to an armoury. She pushed the door open and they entered.

In the centre of the room was a suit of Order armour just like Madeleine was wearing. It shone, bright and powerful.

'Why are we here?' asked Lena.

'Have you been on the battlefield before?' asked the Grandmaster.

'Yes,' Lena replied. 'I was in the vanguard at Castle Winlow.'

'Good.'

The Grandmaster walked over to the nearby wall and took a sword lying there. The sword was much bigger than the swords Lena usually used and without Madeleine's armour helping her, Lena doubted even the Grandmaster could lift it, let alone her.

The Grandmaster turned to Lena. Silas took a step back, understanding what was going on.

It dawned on Lena too. 'Oh no...no, I'm not ready!'

'Lena Faran,' said Grandmaster Madeleine. 'I have heard of your deeds both for your Order and your fellow knights and squires. You have led bravely, looked after them and kept them safe in the face of great danger and adversity. Kneel.'

Lena stopped arguing. She sunk to one knee and bowed her head.

The Grandmaster placed the flat of the sword on one of Lena's shoulders and then the other. 'Lena Faran, on behalf of Grandmaster Alberto and the Order of the Furnace, I name you knight. Arise.'

Lena stood up.

'What do you have to say for yourself?' asked Madeleine.

'Thank you,' said Lena quietly, still not quite believing what had happened. 'I am honoured.'

'Good,' said the Grandmaster. 'It is time for battle and you will make us proud.'

Madeleine turned to Silas.

'Silas, are you prepared to be Lena's armour-bearer for the upcoming battle?'

Silas nodded. 'Of course.'

'Then I will leave you. Meet me back at the great hall once you are ready.'

Madeleine placed the sword back on the rack and left the room.

Lena stared at Silas wide-eyed.

Silas smiled at her. 'Let's get you ready...my lady.'

# Chapter Forty-Three

Nestor entered Oliguer's lair with Berry in his arms and Hounslow ran up to him.

'What's going on?' Hounslow asked.

Nestor looked at Hounslow but he didn't speak. Instead he took Berry over to a table covered in tubes that stood next to Oliguer.

'No,' said Hounslow. 'Not Berry. I thought you were going to get a volunteer? One of the knights here. Berry can't choose this! How can she?'

'It's for the best,' said Nestor. His head was bowed.

'But- but- not Berry!' said Hounslow.

'I'm sorry, my boy,' said Nestor. 'I know you feel for her.'

Hounslow was taken aback. 'What? No- it's just...'

'I've seen how you looked at her while we were travelling here,' said Nestor. He reached out and placed his hand on Hounslow's shoulder. 'I know you sneak into the infirmary every night when you think everyone else is in bed. You're a good boy, Hounslow, but Berry is dying and in doing this she may save us all. I hope you understand.'

Hounslow turned and looked at Berry. 'No...'

Nestor went to the table and picked up a tube and a knife. 'You shouldn't be here for this.'

Hounslow stepped up to the table, wiped Berry's brow and held her hand. He looked at Nestor. 'I should. Do it,' he said.

# Chapter Forty-Four

Lena returned to the great hall in her Order armour. She now stood over six feet tall and the corridors of Fallengarden had echoed with her every step. When she arrived in the great hall Grandmaster Madeleine greeted her.

'You look very impressive, my dear,' said the Grandmaster. 'Now, shall we see what is happening upstairs?'

Lena followed Madeleine to the battlements. There, Lena watched boulders from the Royal Army's catapults smash into Fallengarden's walls and towers and the Order's own weapons firing back at the Royal Army. The noise was tremendous.

Lena looked down at the Royal Army's front line.

'What are they doing?' she asked, pointing at what seemed to be a small group of soldiers who were making their way to Fallengarden's gate house with their shields over their heads.

'Strange,' said the Grandmaster. 'Archers!' she called out. 'The gate, take aim and fire when ready!'

Those on the battlements with bows started shooting at the soldiers. Lena could see the arrows hitting their shields but none of the soldiers fell. Lena watched as the soldiers stood next to the stone blocking the gate house for a time then, suddenly, they bolted, each going their separate ways.

'Looks like we drove them off,' said the Grandmaster.

'Something isn't right-' Lena began, but before she could finish her sentence a huge explosion rocked Fallengarden. Lena and the Grandmaster fell to the ground. When Lena got up again smoke was pouring from the gate.

'What was *that?*' cried Madeleine.

Lena looked to the Royal Army. Something was going on.

The soldiers were all starting to move forward.

'Grandmaster,' said Lena. 'I think they've got through the gates. And if they have something that powerful they could get into the great hall in minutes!'

'Knights!' cried the Grandmaster. 'To the Courtyard! It is time to fight them face-to-face!'

Grandmaster Madeleine and Lena ran down the stairwell from the battlements and through to the great hall. As they went they told everyone they saw what had happened and to get to the platform.

'Knights!' cried the Grandmaster once she had stepped onto the platform. 'The King's army is through our walls and we must hold them back! For Eltsvine and the Orders, victory!'

The knights cheered and Lena joined them.

The platform rose and Lena found herself in Fallengarden's courtyard once again. At the far end smoke was pouring from the ground and she could clearly see a hole where the stone blocking the gate house had been. No royal soldiers had entered yet.

'Line up!' commanded the Grandmaster. 'Position One!'

The Order knights lined up in rows with Lena in the first. The first and second rows brought their shields up and, just like at Castle Winlow, Lena pressed the first button on her shield, uncovering the bolts that hid in its centre-piece.

'Be ready!' cried Grandmaster Madeleine.

At the other end of the courtyard royal soldiers started pouring in through the hole the explosion had made. Lena and the knights of the Order of the Embers waited a few moments more.

'Fire!'

Lena pressed the second button on her shield and the bolts flew forward. The royal soldiers closest to the knights fell to the floor.

'Second row, fire!'

Lena moved to the side and the knights behind Lena pushed their shields forward. Bolts then flew from their shields and more royal soldiers fell.

'Draw!'

Lena pulled her giant sword out of its scabbard. It felt as light as a feather in her gauntleted hand. She reached up and pulled the visor of her helmet down. It clanged shut, and in her armour Lena now felt invincible. Nothing could stop her. She felt like she could fight the Royal Army single-handed and still come out victorious.

'Charge!'

Lena and the other knights burst forward.

# Chapter Forty-Five

The fight had been intense. Lena had crashed into the royal soldiers and started swinging. She was like a demon, cutting her way through the ranks of royal soldiers as if they were barely there. They came at her, but her armour kept their blows from hurting her, and her own sword crushed cuirasses and helmets as if they were made of paper.

Eventually, Lena looked up to see the royal soldiers retreating. She felt exhausted but happy; they had won! They had defeated the Royal Army!

Lena pushed open her visor and smiled at the knight next to her. It was the Grandmaster. 'What are you doing, girl?' shouted the Grandmaster.

'We won!' said Lena.

'Think back to your lessons Lena,' said the Grandmaster. 'If you face a smaller force but they are in a position of strength, what would you do?'

'Wear them down, of course. But- Oh.'

'Exactly.'

Madeleine looked towards the gate house and Lena followed her gaze. Coming through the hole were more soldiers, but these were different to those they had fought already. They were royal knights. The first group had been nothing more than fodder, a means to exhaust Lena and her fellow knights. They weren't expected to win.

The royal knights did not have the same powered armour of the Order of the Embers, but they were strong, covered in plate and were fresh for battle. Lena was suddenly very afraid. She had been stupid to think this would be so easy.

'Regroup!' cried the Grandmaster.

Lena and the Order knights ran back to their lines. They turned to face their new opponents.

Lena watched as the royal knights marched in and formed up. They looked terrifying. Against the royal soldiers Lena had felt like no one could hurt her, but upon seeing the royal knights' swords, she could now imagine one of them bringing her down.

'Let me live through this,' muttered Lena.

'You and me both!' said the knight next to her.

One of the royal knights lifted her sword and brought it down again. The royal knights charged.

# Chapter Forty-Six

Silas stood on the battlements with the other squires. They had bows and fired at the royal knights from above while Lena and the knights of the Embers fought on the ground. Occasionally, a lucky arrow would bring one of the royal knights down, but their armour protected them well. The squires were getting disheartened but they carried on regardless.

Something then caught Silas' eye. One of the Order knights had been cornered by three of the royal knights.

Silas fired a few arrows but they glanced off the royal knights' armour.

'Get away,' cried Silas, but they ignored him.

Suddenly, one of the knights used the pommel of his sword and hit the Order knight in the side of the head. The Order knight fell to the floor and the royal knight reached down and tore the Order knight's helmet off.

It was Lena.

'No!' cried Silas.

He watched as Lena stood back up and fought back, but Silas knew she must have been hurt when her helmet was struck and she looked very tired too.

Silas scanned the courtyard, but all the Order knights were busy in fights of their own. He suddenly had an idea. He left the battlements and ran into the depths Fallengarden, making his way through its corridors until he came to Oliguer's lair. He burst through the doors.

Nestor and Hounslow spun around.

'Silas?' said Nestor. 'Is that you?'

Silas ran to Nestor and Hounslow.

'Lena is in trouble! I need to get to her! I need Alice!'

Nestor looked at Alice.

'She's not really designed to be ridden,' said Nestor. 'And I didn't want her on the battlefield as I have no idea what she might do.'

'Please!' said Silas.

Nestor looked at Alice. She was curled up a few feet away. 'Come here, girl,' he called to her.

Alice got up and padded over. 'Alice,' said Nestor.

'Listen carefully. You need to Take Silas and get Lena back. Don't do anything…unexpected. Do you hear?'

Alice seemed to understand. She walked up to Silas and lowered herself. Silas climbed on her back.

'Thank you,' said Silas, patting Alice. He looked up at Nestor. 'And thank you too.'

'Good luck!' shouted Nestor as Silas and Alice bound out of Oliguer's lair.

Nestor and Hounslow watched Silas and Alice leave.

'How do you think it's going up there?' asked Hounslow. He looked grim and wouldn't take his eyes off Berry.

Nestor shrugged. 'I don't know. But I think it's about to get a lot worse.'

'Because of Alice?'

'Not quite.'

Nestor turned around and looked up, as did Hounslow.

Oliguer roared.

# Chapter Forty-Seven

Silas led Alice up the stairwell until they were on the battlements again. He pointed to where Lena was fighting.

'There!' said Silas.

Alice jumped down from the battlement and Silas held on for dear life. When she landed, she ran towards the royal knights surrounding Lena. Alice crashed into the first, knocking them to the floor. She swiped at the second, tearing their armour open. The royal knights fell back. Silas slid off Alice and went to Lena.

'Are you okay?' Silas asked. He saw Lena was in bad shape. She was bleeding from her head and she had a black eye.

'Yeah,' said Lena. She reached up and touched the cut on her head. 'Just a bit beaten up. Thanks for helping.'

Silas took a bandage from his pack and wound it around Lena's head. 'Don't mention it. I owe you anyway.'

Once her head was bandaged, Lena stood and picked up her sword. She turned to the remaining royal knights nearby and was about to charge them, but none were looking at her or even fighting any more. They were all looking up. The Order knights were now doing the same

'By the Gods,' said a royal knight near Lena. 'What is *that?*'

A shadow now covered the courtyard and the beat of wings filled Lena's ears. On the roof of Fallengarden's keep was a massive machine.

Oliguer stretched out his wings and they filled the sky. He roared and a stream of fire sprang from his mouth, reaching over a hundred feet into the air.

'Run!' cried a royal knight. '*Dragon!*'

Lena and Silas watched, bruised and bloodied, as the Royal Army poured out of Fallengarden's courtyard.

Oliguer took off and swooped over the gatehouse, his wings booming. Lena and Silas ran after the royal knights. On the other side of the gate house they saw Oliguer swoop down and scorch the ground with its breath, turning the Royal Army's siege weapons to cinders.

Lena and Silas watched with their mouths open. Alice padded up to Lena and nuzzled her hand. Lena looked at the mechanical cat.

'And I thought you were scary,' said Lena.

Oliguer changed direction and came back towards Fallengarden once again.

'Is it me or is he coming this way?' said Silas.

Lena and Silas jumped back in fright as Oliguer smashed into the ground in front of them.

Lena could barely speak. She knew how big Oliguer was from seeing him in his lair. Up close, he was breath-taking.

Oliguer turned his head towards the Royal Army. They were all now fleeing in terror, throwing down their weapons in case they slowed them down.

Oliguer roared in triumph once again.

'Thank you!' cried Lena. 'We won! We really won!'

Oliguer turned back to Lena and lowered his head until it was only a few feet away. Suddenly, Oliguer's claw came down and pinned Lena to the ground.

'What are you *doing?*' shouted Lena, fearfully. This wasn't right! Oliguer was on their side! What was going on??

'Do you yield?' rumbled Oliguer.

Lena stopped struggling and looked at Oliguer. 'What?'

'Do you yield, Lena?'

A smile spread across Lena face.

'*Berry?*'

'Surprise,' said Berry.

# Chapter Forty-Eight

A few days after the battle of Fallengarden, Sir Poland, Yvette, and the two knights of the Order of the Embers crested a hill and the Order of the Embers' home came into view.

'Nearly there, my lord,' said one of the knights. He pulled a tube from his cloak and twisted the top. The tube sprung into life, pouring green sparks and smoke into the air. 'We should see a greeting party soon.'

As they continued down onto the plain, Sir Poland could see the ground was both churned and scorched. 'What happened here?'

The second knight shrugged. 'No idea, my lord,' she replied.

Ahead, Sir Poland spotted a group of knights riding out of Fallengarden. At the head of the column were two knights riding Archons and they were in full Order armour. In their hands were two banners: The Order of the Embers and the Order of the Furnace.

When the knights got closer, Sir Poland saw Grandmaster Madeleine was holding her Order's banner.

'Sir Poland!' cried the Grandmaster.

Sir Poland slid off his horse and kneeled, placing his forehead on his knee. 'Grandmaster! You honour me.'

'Get up, Alberghast,' said Grandmaster Madeleine. She slid off her Archon and put out her hand to Sir Poland, who stood and took it joyfully. 'You don't need to be so formal today.'

'My squires,' said Sir Poland. 'Did they get here? And

Nestor? Have you seen him?'

The Grandmaster smiled and looked at the knight holding the Order of the Furnace banner. The knight reached up and took off her helmet.

'Lena!' cried Sir Poland.

'Hello, Milord,' said Lena.

'I thought I'd never see you again!' said Sir Poland. Tears welled in his eyes. 'I am so proud of you!' He looked at Lena's Archon. 'And is that Pandora?' The Archon nuzzled against Sir Poland. 'You made it too, old girl?'

'Good to see you're alive, Alberghast,' said a voice behind Lena.

Sir Poland recognised the voice. Nestor appeared before him. 'Nestor!'

'You're late,' said Nestor with a smile on his face. 'You missed everything. Just like always.'

Grandmaster Madeleine mounted her archon once again. 'Come, Alberghast. There is a great deal to talk about and we have plans to make if we intend to rescue the kingdom. The first step has been made, but there are many others.'

'Of course.' Sir Poland got back on his horse and the party made their way towards Fallengarden. As they rode, Lena told Sir Poland about their journey and the battle that had occurred.

'Berry was hurt?' said Sir Poland. 'That is terrible news. I must see her.'

A terrible cry echoed across the plains and Lena smiled.

'I think she'll want to see you too,' said Lena.

# Epilogue

Erin stood in the throne room of Casenberg Palace. She was dressed in the robes of state and a procession of honour guards stood before her.

'It is time, my lady,' said a nearby attendant. 'They are waiting.'

Erin stepped forward and the honour guard swung into action. They raised their swords and Erin passed underneath them. Once past the guards, she stepped out onto a broad balcony.

Below her, thousands of the residents of Casenberg looked up. Word had spread through the city there was to be a grand announcement and it looked like most of the city had taken an interest.

Erin tried not to smile. It was meant to be a sad day after all. She stood at the balcony edge and raised her hands. The crowd went silent.

'My fellow citizens!' she called out. 'The King is dead!'

There were groans from the crowd and Erin laughed to herself. If only they knew what the King had thought of them.

'The King had no heirs, but fear not,' Erin continued. 'The King, in his infinite wisdom, adopted *me* as his daughter whilst on his death-bed. You all know me well and I know you.' *Much better than you think*, she said to herself. 'I will treat the kingdom well and bring glory to its name! I promise all of you, Eltsvine will be glorious once again!'

The crowd started cheering. It was quiet at first, they were still shocked at the news of their King, no doubt. But soon the cheering got louder and louder.

'Long live Queen Erin! Long live Queen Erin!'

Erin raised her arms once again and the cheering got even louder.

She couldn't hold it back any longer. A smile spread across her face.

*It did not need to be a sad day after all.*

*Lena and Berry will return in:*

# Order of the Furnace Book 2: Justice
ISBN: 9781906132323

*Also by this author:*

# HAYWIRED
## Alex Keller

Ludwig von Guggenstein is about to have his unusual existence turned inside out. When he and his father are blamed for a fatal accident during the harvest, a monstrous family secret is revealed. Soon Ludwig will begin to uncover diabolical plans that span countries and generations while ghoulish machines hunt him down. He must fight for survival, in a world gone haywire.

ISBN: 9781906132330          UK: £7.99

# REWIRED
ISBN: 9781906132347

http://www.mogzilla.co.uk/haywired